Folk's Tales

North Tyneside Writers' Circle

2024

Copyright © 2024 North Tyneside Writers' Circle

All rights reserved.

ISBN: 9798338316665

FOREWORD

Here we are again, North Tyneside Writers' Circle's second anthology, doing it all again for 2024...

North Tyneside Writers' Circle is a free group for writers of all styles, genres and levels of experience, which meets monthly in North Shields Library on the third Saturday of every month except December. We have a range of activities, including responding to writing prompts, sharing our news, successes and opportunities, and having discussions on key topics, often selected by the group.

Our first collection, *Black Coals, White Sands*, was released in autumn 2023, and happily, the process was enough fun that everyone wanted to do it again!

This year, members voted to write on the theme of 'folk', and as with last year, that's taken us in a wonderful range of directions. From folk music to folk tales, through to tales of everyday folk going about their lives, there's something for everyone in this collection.

Again, I'm incredibly grateful to the Editorial Committee, who helped with editing (it would be odd if they didn't!), cover-design and structure of the collection. I honestly could not do this without them.

NTWC is always open to new members; do find us on Facebook and get in touch.

As with last year, we hope you enjoy reading this collection as much as we've enjoyed writing it and putting it together.

Jennifer C. Wilson, September 2024

CONTENTS

The Ballad of NTWC by Bea Charles 1

The Demon Rabbit of Newcastle by James A. Tucker . 3

Folk Club by Harry Gallagher 8

Folkie Blokey by Harry Gallagher 9

Session Watchers by Harry Gallagher.................... 10

Folk Session by Harry Gallagher.......................... 11

Pataloto by Penny Blackburn 12

Hiraeth by Missi Currier 18

A Conspiracy of Proof by Jennifer C. Wilson 23

It's In The Blood by Jennifer C. Wilson 27

The Secret Landing of Sedna by Jennifer C. Wilson .. 28

The Lucky Ones by Jessica Arragon...................... 29

Lunch by Ross Punton 33

Maypole Dancers by Ross Punton........................ 35

Welcome to the Interdimensional Impound by Ross Punton... 36

The Leprechaun's Lament by Ross Punton 38

Time Machines by Wayne Medford...................... 39

The Monolith by Joss Hancock........................... 42

Bandstand by Renata Connors 47

Let Me Tell You About The Hedley Kow by Alexi Calamity 48

Not Entirely A Hero by Arthur J. Montieth 51

Folk Should Not Bring Spirits by Alison Sidney 55

No Wedding and a Funeral by Alison Sidney............ 56

Don't Talk to Strangers by Bridget Gallagher 58

Lost Treasures by Jenny Smith 62

From Cullercoats to North Shields – Following the herring by Jenny Smith 63

Outfoxed by Chris Longstaff 67

Miss Jones by Pureheart Wolf............................ 72

Home is Where the Folk Reside by Pureheart Wolf ... 73

The Search for Scottish Giants by A.R. Cole 74

Juggling with Cynthia Neptune by Noreen Rees 79

Gig Tale by Steve Lancaster 82

Evensong by Steve Lancaster 87

The Book by Elizabeth Drabble........................... 88

Contributors 92

Folk's Tales

Folk's Tales

THE BALLAD OF NTWC

To be sung tunelessly, with a finger inserted in one ear. (For those of a sensitive disposition, a finger in both ears is recommended.)

Let me tell you the tale of the North Tyneside Writers,
The circular crew who meet monthly.
Safe in their den, with keyboard, pencil and pen,
At the library in North Shields they gather.

They are led by an outlaw, so fearless and bold,
Wor Jen she is known and is feared.
She has visions of ghosts, (King Richard, she boasts),
And her novels are rightly applauded.

This Circle of writers, they gather and talk
without pausing for breath or to listen,
'Til Jen speaks, and they cease,
for none will oppose Wor Jen, to whom reverence is given.

Her prompts, they are fiendish, and writers they dread
what fresh torment she plans to inflict.
She commands and they write, imaginations take flight,
But they stop when she calls 'It is time!'

Then see how they offer, so eager to read
what they've written, her favour to win.
Their writing concise ('cos her timer's precise),
Inspired prose, free writing, and rhyme.

Like folk heroes of old, North Tyneside's tales will be told
long after their time here has passed.
But the best known of all, the name we'll recall,
Is Wor Jen, the Circle's top lass.

Folk's Tales

So gather around, young writers and old,
Be there in North Shields next month.
They'll inspire you to tell your stories reet well,
Join Wor Jen and the North Tyneside bunch!

Bea Charles

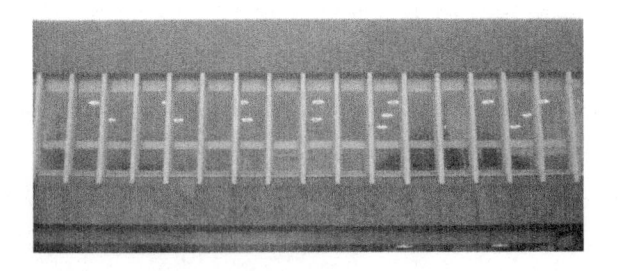

Folk's Tales

THE DEMON RABBIT OF NEWCASTLE

Gather round and prick up your ears, an' I'll tell you how your great-grandparents defeated the Demon Rabbit of Newcastle.

If you're still giggling by the end George, you'll be a fine, brave boy. The Demon Rabbit's hundreds of years old and it's eaten bigger children than you.

Oh, is that so, little Miss Clever Clogs? No rabbits before there were potatoes? No, it wasn't a hare, either. People been bringing rabbits over ever since the Romans, but most of them died, they couldn't handle the cold. In the end they got tougher until they could. Demon rabbit got too tough.

You haven't heard of it because it's too scary, see? Didn't get dealt with centuries ago like the Lambton Worm, and it doesn't just scare you or mess about like ghosts. That man from Monty Python, he knew the legend, he's a proper scholar.

They say it all started because of one of them mean medieval lords. I won't say who it was because his descendants might be canny people, and I'm not sure you can believe it anyway, not like you can believe my part of the story.

This baron was coming home from a long trip. Dare say he had his armour on, and that'd make anyone grumpy. He was riding along when he came to a hut with a rabbit in a cage, and an old woman sitting next to it. Now rabbits were very rare in them days and people thought they were a fine delicacy. These days we just think they're full of bones, but the baron's mouth watered.

"Give me that rabbit!" he said. Dare say he could have paid for it, but he didn't want to.

"That rabbit's my only meat, I'll starve without it," said the old woman. "Have pity!"

The baron was used to taking what he wanted, and he reckoned he could just accuse the woman of black magic if there was any trouble. So he knocked her over, took the rabbit, broke its neck and put it in his bag.

Folk's Tales

"I hope the rabbit eats you instead!" croaked the old woman from the floor. The baron thought this was the stupidest parting shot he'd ever heard, and went on his way laughing.

Only maybe she had been a witch, or perhaps something else heard her… because later, when the servants set a big pot down in front of him and removed the lid, what did he see inside? Sat in the boiling gravy was a very different kind of rabbit. It was bigger and it was the colour of a pot bottom that's been on fires for longer than you've been alive. Its ears stood on end, and they were as sharp as leaf-blade swords. Its eyes were huge, and they glowed red like those coals at the bottom of our fire. It opened its mouth and instead of rabbit teeth, it had huge fangs. It put its feet up on the side of the pot and they weren't round paws, they were long and bony with claws just as sharp as the fangs.

Then it jumped out and ate the lord right up. Well, it was a magic rabbit, its stomach was a lot bigger than it was! Its hide was like iron and it was strong as a bear, it drove the men-at-arms away with dreadful injuries. When it had finished, it left the bones and hopped away into the night.

But that wasn't the end of it. The rabbit kept ravaging the countryside around. Ravaging is like savaging only more medievil, right? It ate anything it found outside after dark. That was mostly animals, because people learned sharpish to be behind bolted doors before the sun went down. The only peace they had was in daytime or in winter, because it hated the cold. When the frosts started coming it would tunnel right down near to Hell where it was warm; they'd find a burrow with brimstone smoke coming out of it, and they'd heave a sigh of relief.

Brimstone… well alright I don't know, but it smells like eggy farts. Stop giggling. This is serious.

People tried to hunt the rabbit, but dogs and cats were scared of it. The bravest knights of the land said they had better things to do than fight a rabbit, so they weren't that brave after all.

Folk's Tales

So instead the monks of Lindisfarne got a huge rock, blessed it with many prayers, and put it over the top of the rabbit's hole one winter. That did the trick... at least until the year of 1910. There were loads of new buildings going up, someone must have found the rock and dug it out without knowing why it was there.

Demon rabbits don't starve or get old. Maybe it had got a little weaker, because it didn't kill anyone at first, but the streets of the Toon became ones of terror.

My father, Bill, was a young policeman at the time. The other coppers didn't believe what was happening, they thought it must be some kind of rabid dog and everyone who saw it was drunk or mad. But Bill knew the legend, and he was lucky because he had a clever sweetheart called Pat.

She went off to the Literary and Philosophical Society to make a plan. It was full of very grand ladies and gentlemen smoking pipes and reading or writing away, but they knew what was what, so they helped her all they could.

Pat read local folklore. She noticed the rabbit always avoided sunlight. Then she wondered if they needed supernatural help of their own. The Cauld Lad of Hylton was closest, but he was cruel to cats, so she didn't like the sound of him.

Then she spotted something useful. There was a spirit at Black Heddon called Silky, because of her dress. She was scary, but never did people any real harm. The special thing about her was that she had a power over animals; she could freeze horses in their tracks, turn them around or send them in a panic, and liked to play her tricks at a local bridge.

Trouble was that Silky hadn't been seen for a while, not since a load of gold had been found in the roof of a house. Folk reckon she'd become a ghost because of being a miser when she was alive, so tight she could "peel an orange in her pocket" as they say around here.

Well, Pat and Bill reckoned they had a way to get her attention; they'd dig a hole and bury something valuable near her bridge at night. Best they could do was the bank-book of Bill's father, which they borrowed without telling him. Just as they were shovelling soil on it, the ghost appears right behind them and gives them a hell of a shock. She doesn't look as ugly as the stories.

"You don't want to do that; you might get stuck as a ghost until it's found!" says Silky.

They tell her why they're there. Silky's happy to help, she's been bored while she's been at rest.

The next night, they spring their trap. The Demon Rabbit is easy to find because it's so nasty that it doesn't hide from anything. So it gets a big shock when Bill shoots it in the head with a slingshot. It spins round and it's about to rip him to pieces, when up pops Silky and does her trick.

Silky can paralyse a whole team of horses, but she can't do more than just slow the rabbit down, to about the speed a man can run. So Bill sprints as fast as he can and the rabbit chases after him, lighting up the street with its blazing eyes, ripping up cobbles with its claws. Silky gets dragged along after it.

They reach St Nick's Cathedral and Bill falls down tired, round the back where they're building new offices. The rabbit gets on top of a door ready to jump on him for the kill, but then Pat starts ringing the church bells. She's not very tuneful but it doesn't matter. Church bells are good against bad supernatural things, and together with Silky, that finally stops the rabbit dead.

Now the rabbit realises it's nearly daybreak, and it's in real trouble. It howls defiance at the sky like a wolf. But the sun comes up and when its light touches the rabbit, it turns to stone.

Well, they had some explaining to do, but enough people knew the old legends that our heroes got a vote of thanks and folk always did 'em favours after that. Silky went back to sleep and people said prayers for her. Bill and Pat married and had wonderful, fine children. Even their great-grandchildren are canny when they go to bed on time.

As for the rabbit... you can still see it there.

James A. Tucker

Folk's Tales

FOLK CLUB

It's a dying art,
this communion.
In a slabcold room
we cluster for warmth,
serenade old comrades
fallen from the road,
sing our old songs,
each of us looking
a touch more worn
than last we checked.

Tentative as finches,
we reach for harmonies,
breadcrumbs, fairydust
we once took as ours.

Yet once in a while
a line winds its way
into a place,
deep and forgotten
as a memory of love.

Tearducts are squeezed,
soft peachy cheeks
dabbed with handkerchiefs
clean as when mother
rinsed them for Sunday
morning church.

We sing, find ways
to remember anew
what we had forgotten
when the world was new.

Harry Gallagher

FOLKIE BLOKEY

When I were a lad,
a folkie was someone
my Dad's age. Clad
in Arran's best, belly
bigger than chest,
finger in ear, hand
welded to beer glass.

They sang of fair maidens
down in the valley-o.
Mixing warm ales with
tales of the dales.
Leftover crusts
and yesterday's baccy
embedded in beard-o.

And now here am I
frightening the horses
with not-so-close harmonies –
all the right notes
in all the wrong keys.

Reading my sepia lines,
locked in the land
of blast furnaces and mines;
but the times,
they are still a-changing.

Harry Gallagher

Folk's Tales

SESSION WATCHERS

you see them drift in
asif on a sirocco,
dreaming on their feet

they were just passing by,
pulled in by the ears
then held by the heart

later falling to bed
they tell tall tales
of having seen brigadoon

how it's made from a heal,
the wounds they bore
having all disappeared

and how they were carried
alltheway home
on a bed of the softest notes

                                                    Harry Gallagher

FOLK SESSION

Somenights the jigs an' reels
take the beater from your fingers
and spin it round the room
like a dolly on acid
and the counting just happens,
comes through a window.

Somenights thirds an' fifths
are accompanied by sevenths
and the brethren gathered
all sup from the same glass,
which is misted with magic
and all the prophets hold dear.

And somenights, just somenights
tablelegs leave their station
and paddle in the joy
of a session gone native.

Harry Gallagher

PATALOTO

There was once—in a long ago land, in a far away time—a man named Conrad, who lived in a tiny whitewashed cottage on the edge of a village. Conrad lived by gleaning grain from the fields and he grew vegetables in the patch of earth beside his cottage. Generally, he considered himself a lucky man, for he had also fresh eggs from his chickens and crisp apples from the tree beside his door. When he heard of anyone ailing in the village, he sent along a basket of eggs, and he always had spare apples for the local children. He helped his neighbours with odd jobs and in return they gave him a little meat or wine and so he had just enough to get by.

Now, as well as the hens that laid his eggs, Conrad also had a rooster, a wise animal named Pataloto. Every morning Conrad would call to the bird:

Pataloto, Pataloto, fine and fair
Pataloto, Pataloto, bring me something rare

Pataloto would crow loudly and scratch at the earth—under the apple tree or around the vegetable beds—to see what he could find. Some days there was nothing, but sometimes there might be a lucky hagstone, or a shell from an ancient sea, or a bone that Conrad could make into a whistle. Whatever Pataloto found, Conrad would thank him and put it somewhere safe.

Mostly Conrad was happy, but sometimes after supper he would look into the fire and become melancholy.

"Ah, Pataloto," he would sigh, "The thatch is nearly bare and the walls are crumbling. I work hard all day long, but there is never enough left over to make a difference. How can I ever improve my lot?"

"Master, do not fear," Pataloto would reply. "The world will turn again and things may change."

"Indeed," Conrad would reply, patting the bird. "You speak wise words." And that, for a time, would be the end of the matter.

One bright morning at the start of spring, Conrad called to Pataloto as always:

Pataloto, Pataloto, fine and fair
Pataloto, Pataloto, bring me something rare

And Pataloto crowed and scratched the soil and turned up a shining gold coin that dazzled in the sunlight. Conrad gasped. He blinked his eyes. Then he shouted for joy, "Pataloto, you fine creature! Look what you have found!"

Pataloto crowed louder than ever, until all the village came to see what the noise was for. The coin was passed around and marvelled at and Conrad thought himself the luckiest man alive. Here would be enough to fix the roof and render the walls, maybe enough buy a bigger piece of land, some sheep—what a wonder!

But there are no secrets where there are mouths and so within a few days Conrad was summoned to take his coin to the King. After waiting at the palace gates, a servant finally led him through a maze of corridors and into a grand room, decorated in velvet and damask and lit by crystal chandeliers. At the centre was the King, sitting on a high, elaborate throne, surrounded by his advisors. Conrad swallowed hard as the servant ushered him before the throne.

"Who are you?" demanded the King.

An advisor stepped forward and whispered in the King's ear, passing him Conrad's coin. The King smiled, but not in a kindly way.

"Ah yes, the man who found a coin."

Again the advisor stepped forward. The King frowned.

"I see. The man whose *rooster* found a coin." Disdain dripped from his voice.

Conrad nodded, not knowing what to reply.

Folk's Tales

"Is this a common occurrence?" snapped the King. "Your bird *finding things*?"

Conrad nodded again. "Yes, sometimes he—"

"Then what he finds you shall bring to me. Everything. Do you understand?"

Conrad nodded for a third time.

"May I have my coin back?"

But the King waved his hand dismissively and Conrad was led from the room.

"Well, what a situation!" Conrad said to Pataloto that night. "Now I have no coin and the King wants everything you find. What a palaver indeed!"

Pataloto cocked his feathered head. "Not to worry, master. You must follow the King's instructions, but will you also follow mine as well?"

"Of course I will, Pataloto. What must I do?"

"Just leave everything to me. Call me in the morning as usual."

So the next morning, Conrad rose and called to Pataloto as always:

Pataloto, Pataloto, fine and fair
Pataloto, Pataloto, bring me something rare

Pataloto crowed loudly and scratched at the earth and turned up a stone, smooth and polished and the shape of a heart. As instructed by the King, Conrad took it straight to the palace.

"What is this rubbish?" sneered the King.

"Why sire, it is what Pataloto found this morning. Is it not marvellous?" These were the words his rooster had told him to say, and he followed the instruction carefully.

"Marvellous?" gasped the King. "It is no such thing!"

"But sire, how wonderful that nature should create such a perfect symbol of love! What treasure!"

"It is no treasure to me!" replied the King. "Do not bring me worthless things. Bring me precious metals, jewellery and such. Be gone!"

So Conrad left, taking his heart-shaped stone with him.

The next morning, Conrad repeated his ritual:

Pataloto, Pataloto, fine and fair
Pataloto, Pataloto, bring me something rare

And this time the bird turned up an old fork, missing all but one of its tines and bent out of shape.

"Take it to the King," instructed Pataloto.

"This old thing?" asked Conrad. "He will be furious."

"Do as *he* instructs. Do as *I* instruct," replied the bird, so Conrad headed once more to the palace.

The King seethed as he examined the fork.

"This is worse than yesterday's offering. What am I to do with it?"

Conrad again spoke the words Pataloto had told him to.

"Sire, I am a poor and humble man. I was told to bring what I find, and I do not know which metals are precious and which are not. It grieves me that this treasure is not to your liking."

The King thrust the fork abruptly back at him.

"Take it away. Bring me something better tomorrow."

So for a third day, Conrad called to Pataloto to see what he would find:

Pataloto, Pataloto, fine and fair
Pataloto, Pataloto, bring me something rare

This time when Pataloto scratched, he upturned a small blue glass bead about the size of a grain of barley.

"Take it to the King," said Pataloto, "and speak the words I tell you."

Conrad felt the King's anger as he took the tiny bead in his hand.

"What the blazes is *this*?" he roared.

Conrad trembled before the King's rage, but he kept Pataloto's words in his mind and spoke them clearly.

"Sire, it is a precious jewel."

"This is no kind of jewel. It has no value, no worth."

"But sire, it was created by the skill of an artisan glass blower. That a man can turn sand and ash and stone into something so delicate is surely something to be treasured?"

"Ach! You are a fool! You and your bird are a waste of my time. I will have no more of it. You are never to bother me again."

"And if I find something else of value, sire?"

"You do not know value from a hole in the ground. I do not want anything you find."

Conrad remembered Pataloto's last instruction. He braved the King's wrath once more.

"Sire, will you put in writing that I am to keep what I find? I do not wish people to think I would dare to disobey your order."

"Very well," agreed the king, beckoning forward an advisor. "It shall be done, and you shall never trouble me again."

"Indeed, sire," replied Conrad.

So Conrad went home and carried on as before and was happy when Pataloto turned up hagstones and beads and shells and old bones. And he would take great delight in looking at his letter from the King which decreed that anything Pataloto found was Conrad's to keep. He was especially delighted on the day when the bird turned up the rest of the bag of gold coins from which the first one had come.

From then on Conrad and Pataloto lived in comfort, with a well-thatched roof and sturdy walls. They had more than enough to buy what they needed, so Conrad didn't have to work quite so hard and he spent time teaching the village children to make whistles from old bones and the village was filled with music and laughter.

And while Conrad was not the kind of man who would want to sleep in a golden bed with feather eiderdowns, it is certain that for the rest of his life Pataloto slept at his side on the plumpest velvet cushion that money could buy.

Penny Blackburn

HIRAETH

The city was awash in blurred monochrome from TV static sky as the rain lashed down on her commute. It was a dawnless morning. No kiss of sunrise, just the world transitioning from black to dark grey that showed no hope of improving. The kind of weather that her nana would say had "set in."

She was already full of at least five regrets, four of them to do with her choice of footwear for such a day, and the other for not just phoning in sick altogether. She made a conscious effort to straighten her back, determined to correct her slouch after her mother commented that she looked like a croissant on Insta. The rain at least brought the small pleasure of using the automatic opening function on her umbrella. At the touch of a button, she became a powerful witch queen as its red cover spiralled upwards like flamenco skirts into the gloom. These little daydreams kept her heart beating.

This wasn't the quickest way to work, but for her, it was the only way. Rush hour bus journeys do not allow space to dream.

It was five years since she started feeding the crows there. She remembered this distinctly because it was the day she started taking the tablets. There was a clear correlation between these two events. The pills caused her to feel disgusted by food, but the instructions advised against taking them without eating. Her brain made a deal with her stomach, tempting it with two Babybel lights. As she passively picked at the thin ribbon of the cheese, she noticed a crow skipping hopefully alongside her and gladly surrendered the snack to it, delighted at the careful way he used his beak to remove the wax. She named him Djinn, and his smaller mate, Tonic, quickly joined their dynamic. Their symbiotic connection enchanted her days ever since. The crows got snacks, and she found a tiny gap in time she could rest in. The pause at the top of a rollercoaster where she could gaze at the view before hurtling back down the hill towards the urgency of modern life. Up here, she felt a sense of clarity and simplicity in her purpose. Down there, success was measured by APRs, alarms, fitness app streaks, and praise from an animated green owl she feared would spring from her phone and roundhouse kick her to the jaw if she forgot to practice her Irish that day. These vapid achievements were the things that she pretended made her a functional human being. Connection had less to do with empathy and more to do with internet speed.

Reaching the park, she removed her headphones, muting the soothing voice of the American therapist reading her mindfulness affirmations. Djinn flew down from the parking meter first, prompting his brethren to follow. He was bolder and more curious than the rest. The sound of his wings cutting the air past her ear echoed a familiar whoosh, reminding her of the little sound her phone made whenever she sent an email. A strange clinking noise accompanied Djinn's arrival, his claw revealing a miniature glass rum bottle, reminiscent of the souvenirs her aunt always brought back from trips.

As she dished out the monkey nuts, listening for the soothing crack of shells in beaks, she was aware of a woman watching them in her periphery, waiting for her chance to interrupt.

"You could tame them, you know?" she said. "I bet within a year you could train them to sit on your shoulder."

The younger woman's eye twitched. She practiced a few diaphragmatic breaths that she had learned through the employee assistance program. It promised to help her regulate her overwhelming irritation when forced into social interactions, but was yet to yield results.

She knew the woman meant no harm. If she was honest, that had been a secret goal of hers in the beginning, though she hated to admit it. That's ego and loneliness for you. To possess the inner purity and charm that makes strange animals trust you, and have others envy the bonds you form with them. But there's no authentic connection in that. She never wanted these birds to fully trust any human, including herself. It would keep them safe and free. Why wouldn't you want the crows to teach you to be wild? To show her how to leap from the cliffs and dance with the thermals just for the thrill.

Instead of vocalising this, she deployed a dad joke to swerve further conversation.

"I wish they'd teach me to fly off somewhere a bit sunnier," she said, then pretended to take a swig from her tiny bottle while wishing to every old god that she could unshackle herself from civility and small talk forever. If her attention hadn't been focused on the woman's scrutiny, she would have noticed Djinn's head tilt and the orphic rattle from his throat as he conspired with destiny.

She thought nothing of the itching in her eye while at work that day. Coupled with office noise and light sensitivity, she assumed she had another migraine coming on. Walking home, her senses spiked. She noticed the dance of every cherry blossom petal that sashayed down the road in the Beltane breeze. Silver threads descending from the trees stole her attention, adorned with tiny caterpillars, swaying like trapeze artists. The murmur of the water in the pipes beneath bellowed like Gregorian chants. As a robin darted out from a tiny gap in a privet hedge, her eyes fixed on its tiny nest within. Inside, a clutch of perfect, teal eggs sat in a cradle of moss and feathers. The compulsion to snatch one had already defibrillated from her brain to her fingers before her conscience could stop her. The egg felt warm in the coolness of her palm for a few seconds, before she urgently stuffed it into her mouth and bared down on the calcified crunch of brittle shell. She had expected to vomit, but the rich yolk was like ambrosia to her. As she prepared to help herself to another, the robin returned and unleashed the full fury of its grief toward her eyes, tiny claws and feather blades slashing at her face. She fled the scene, her eyes darting around to check for the twitch of nets in the suburbs.

Upon entering the house, she immediately rushed to the mirror. Her eye appeared slightly darker than usual, but nothing seemed obviously wrong. Within hours, her skin broke in a burning rash and unusual pimple-like structures covered her face. Mistaking it for a blackhead, she squeezed one of the larger ones on the bridge of her nose. To her surprise, the thick, dark keratin unexpectedly separated, revealing a perfect, tiny feather.

She resolved to call in sick tomorrow. The company placed high value on appearances. Visible tattoos and piercings were grounds for dismissal. Corporate policy didn't cover facial feathers, but the imaginary conversation with HR that played in her head was enough to inform her decision. Over the next few hours, more pin feathers broke through her skin. She knew she should have called someone for help, but felt strangely titillated by the sensation. Until the pain set in. Her body spasmed as bone and muscle contorted and screamed like a plane crash.

The last thing she heard before losing consciousness was the sound of her vertebrae cracking as her spine straightened. On wakening, she felt profound relief in the dark and stillness within her body. The room felt too large, though. She knew whatever had happened was impossible and permanent. Walking to the bedside table, she looked up at her phone in its charging stand. The screen remained dark as the biometric lock failed to recognise her new form. Its smooth glass acting as an obsidian mirror, allowing her to take in the transformation that had occurred. She slowly stretched one wing, marvelling at the beautiful and vibrant colours that shimmered in the moonlight. For the first time in her life, she felt both beautiful and vital.

Sudden tapping on the window nearly caused her tiny heart to come through her chest, and as she turned her head, she was relieved to find Djinn standing by the open window. Knowing she had seen him, he took flight, glancing behind his shoulder as if beckoning her to follow. Leaping clumsily onto the windowsill, she absorbed the repainted world before her. She felt the tingle of starlight on her tongue. She saw the sky and all the galaxies that lay beyond it. This night did not look like the ones where she walked home with her keys between her fist. It did not look like the where ones she lay awake, dreading the first strip of dawn. As she arched her wings, she

Folk's Tales

left the last burdens of human thought on the ledge, lifted her beak to the night like a kiss, and threw herself into the dark violet iridescence of love.

Missi Currier

A CONSPIRACY OF PROOF

The dates had been in the diary for months: 26th and 27th August 2023. It was widely advertised across the news, social media, and naturally, whispered about in bars, hotels, and cafés along the shores of a certain loch.

And of course, she hears it.

Just as she is meant to.

She hears, she pays attention, and she plans.

Just as she is meant to.

On Saturday morning, the loch's shores and surface are alive with activity. Drones with infra-red cameras buzz in the skies, a hydrophone is lowered into the dark, and volunteers from the Loch Ness Exploration research team line every safe vantage point.

Everything is set for two whole days of investigation, the biggest single search effort since the Loch Ness Investigation Bureau's work in 1972.

The results of this extensive scientific campaign?

Four unidentified 'gloops'. And the sound equipment wasn't recording at the time. (It wasn't even switched on.)

After that? Nothing. Not one sighting, no more gloops, not even a disturbance on the loch's stunning surface, which could have potentially been attributed to their target.

Let's be honest, there was never going to be. Clever old Nessie, letting the researchers have their four precious gloops. Still, she knew the equipment would never have recorded them, as she sat still, so still, below the hydrophone-carrying vessel. She may not be able to communicate directly back to her important shore-based contacts, but everyone knows the signs, and she knew fine-well one of her co-conspirators would be on that boat, 'accidentally' forgetting to check the recording device was running.

That one special little beach, tucked so out of the way in woodlands that you really cannot stumble across it by accident, that's where the magic happens. It's strange, passing messages on to a prehistoric plesiosaur; for one thing, it took a while to work out which language to use. And who to trust.

After the first 'modern day' sightings in the 1870s, a small band of locals decided that, given the prevalence of hunting in the Scottish Highlands, if there was something in the water, it deserved a chance to survive and thrive, not become the latest trophy on a castle wall. So they began scouring the loch's edge, calling quietly at night, trying a combination of Scottish Gaelic, a bit of Irish Gaelic (this creature, or its kin, had been spotted by St Columba, after all), and modern English.

Success, when it came, was equally terrifying and exhilarating, as a long, graceful neck rose out of the water at the beach.

"They're hunting for you," the locals warned. "You need to stay hidden." This latter warning was accompanied by an odd, but clearly effective form of interpretive dance / creative mime.

It took a few attempts, but eventually, with an incline of its head, the creature seemed to understand.

"We are friends," the creature was informed, repeatedly, the point emphasised by gifts of food (this was also a case of trial and error, until the sweet treat of flowers (lavender and chamomile being her favourites) was confirmed as the best option). "Trust us, not others."

And so it began.

That small group kept up their role, handing the secret down from generation to generation, never letting it leave their loyal band, determined to keep 'their Nessie' safe. There was talk of refusing to use the name she had been given by the world at large, nothing more than a shortening of her home, but in the end, why confuse things? If she heard herself being referred to as something different, she may make a mistake, misunderstand what she was being told.

When one of the current generation of Nessie's loyal protectors became an employee of the Scottish Tourist Board; that's when the debate started.

The question they had to consider was: now the threat of hunting was over, should Nessie show herself to the world? Or should the mystery be maintained?

Even with the rarity of sightings (or possible sightings; good old ripples and seiches), there were full boat-trips and vantage points lined with tourists. There were Nessie-themed restaurants, cafés, and gift-shops. Campsites were popping up in spare fields. There were souvenirs.

Ultimately, the myth was far more tantalising. After all, there's more kudos to seeing something that may or may not exist than something that appears every other day and wows the crowds. Nessie would maintain her seclusion, keep herself from the world as much as she could.

And so, even with the rarity of sightings, there ARE full boat-trips and vantage points lined with tourists. There ARE Nessie-themed restaurants, cafés, and gift-shops. Campsites ARE popping up in spare fields. There ARE souvenirs.

Our merry band of conspirators were correct: the myth and mystique were far more valuable than the guarantee.

Naturally, over the years, it's become an obsession for some to try and find her, with the 1972 campaign being one example, and the 1987 three-day scientific hunt, with its multi-boat sonar 'net'. Mind, that one did come close, too close, to be honest. Three positive sonar contacts were recorded during one sweep of the loch, which were suspiciously not present when the boat returned to the exact location a short while later. Thank goodness she got out the way in time.

That's the way it works these days. She'll always give just enough evidence to keep her myth going, but never enough for it to be proven either way. You can't prove a negative, after all.

Of course, the tourist board are well-versed in things now, though they'll never let on. Why would they? I shouldn't even be telling you this. I'm one of Nessie's gang, you see. I don't work in tourism officially; well, I suppose I do, technically—we all do, if you think about it. Without our collaboration, who knows what would have happened to the lovely Family Ness (yes, we know the cartoon, and we love it). Would she have ended up as merely a trophy? Captured and dragged into an aquarium? Dissected and displayed as nothing but bones? It doesn't bear thinking of. This way, she's safe, Scotland's tourism industry maintains its greatest star, and we enjoy the satisfaction of keeping one of the world's most glorious secrets.

Don't get me wrong, we're not immune to the tourism nonsense.

Which is why, if you'll excuse me, I must get back to work. Those Nessie figurines aren't going to make themselves...

Jennifer C. Wilson

IT'S IN THE BLOOD

There is a theory that summoning sea creatures,
drawing them from their oceanic dwellings,
comes naturally, still, to some humans.
To the ones within which the blood still runs saline,
for whom dilution hasn't hit.
It's most common, most natural, for the coast-dwellers;
the ones who haven't strayed (couldn't) too far from our aquatic origins.
We don't even know we're doing it, not really;
there's just a gentle pull, or push,
just as the ebbs and flow of the tide,
bringing us to the shore, time after time.

If this doesn't feel like you, have no fear;
there's space on this earth for us all.
But if you're more at home on land than on water,
there are signs you can use, to spot the others –
the ones with saltwater running strong in their veins…

Are they luckier than most, when seeking sea-life?
Are they always the first to spot a seal?
(Are you completely sure it is just a seal?)
Are they naturally drawn to rockpools,
where they always, ALWAYS find the good critters?
And when you go for a paddle, in that sparkling blue,
are you sure there isn't just a hint of webbing?

Jennifer C. Wilson

THE SECRET LANDING OF SEDNA

She calls on the Qualupalik,
summoning them to come, prevent
the villagers approaching the shore,
and begs Sila to hold her breath,
pausing the Great North Wind.
Only then will Sedna emerge,
drying her moon-kissed skin
on Nanook's warming fur.

Teikkeitsertok keeps watch,
his caribou standing guard,
but there are no witnesses here now.
The birds who could spread this tale
are long gone, south,
to escape night's chilling grasp.
So, Sedna sleeps, and dreams,
lullabied by her sea canaries,
waiting belugas, ready
for when their mistress's rest is done.

Jennifer C. Wilson

THE LUCKY ONES

As children we are genetically programmed to seek the approval of our folks. We want to make them proud. We want to share our victories with them and have them celebrate proudly with us. We want them to comfort and reassure us when we're feeling sad. We want them to give us strength when our own is diminishing. We need them to provide safety. We need to grow up with the absolute certainty that if the world was burning, they would open their door, fight through the flames, and grant us sanctuary. And as the sparks fly and the world burns and the sky is a fiery inferno, we are secure. We sleep soundly, safe in the knowledge that we are wrapped in a protective bubble of love so strong, so deep, so resilient and unconditional, that not even the hottest of hell fires could permeate it. Wouldn't that be something?

Some children, the lucky ones, are born to mothers who glow in pregnancy, whose hearts swell with the promise of life growing and moving inside them. Those mothers imagine what the child will look like, what colour her eyes will be. Certain that it's a girl, they imagine dressing her in pink and braiding her hair into French plaits. They already love her fiercely, unconditionally. They clutch their bellies, desperate to embrace their little one, even before she's taken a breath. They will be her cheerleader, her confidante, her teacher, her protector. They imagine the nightly feeds, the baby's head snuggled against them, so closely that not even a piece of paper could pass between them. The smell of the crown of their daughter's head is intoxicating. It activates something primal in them, animalistic. It reinforces, unequivocally, the sacred bond between them. And it binds them to the man they made her with. They know, without doubt, that their role is to love, care for, and protect this little one above anything else.

But what if your mother did not feel any of that? Not when you were an innocent flutter in the womb. Not even when you were placed in her arms, having been torn from her belly. What if she was incapable of it? What if every interaction you shared confirmed that to you both? What if even before you were capable of language you sensed that indifference? What if it wasn't love that greeted you upon entering the world, but resentment? While some mothers receive a bundle of joy, yours got a lump of concrete chained to her foot. And worse still, a lump that's the mirror image of the man she's shackled to.

Growing up I learned that less is definitely more. I shared little and was criticised for being secretive. But I needed to be. Sharing anything that was important to me resulted in ridicule. I did well in school? I was a teacher's pet. I did less well in school? 'They' should bring back the Dunce's Hat, that would teach me! I read too much. I talked too little. I had my head in the clouds. I was forever in the way. I disgusted you when I ate. I was dirty. Nothing I did ever met with your expectations. I tried to ask your opinion on things that mattered to me, and you wouldn't even look up to give me an answer. You would just provide a bland response that told me nothing other than you hadn't listened to me in the first place.

Punishment was dished out freely and unjustly. I didn't even always know what I'd done to displease you. Existed perhaps? I learned to read the room. Slight shifts in the atmosphere presaged the likelihood of an explosion. I learned to act fast and get the hell out of Dodge before things really got spicy…

Thanks for that, by the way. It's a 'talent' that I've kept all these years. I can sense feelings in others better than I can feel them in myself. No sense in crying, or you'll get something to cry for. Thanks to you, I can sense the full spectrum of emotions in others, whereas inwardly I have the emotional capability of a triangle. Rigid, fixed, with three dominant emotions. You won't be surprised to hear that one of them is anger, one is sadness, and the other is the childish excitement that you stole from me, and my children gifted back to me. The only time I know I'm feeling something is when my heart beats so fast and my chest is so tight I can't breathe. Thanks for that too. It really helped me to develop a sense of pragmatism and rationale. It really helped me to hone my logical thinking. No, really, it's served me well. You would be so proud…

I looked at some mood cards the other day. There's at least 42 emotions. 42! And you wouldn't let me feel any of them. Cheers! Good parenting.

For years I sought your approval. For years I thought I needed you to be proud of me. I expected you to encourage me, but your stock answer was to tell me to give up. You criticised my decisions, my life choices. Confusingly, despite my relative success, no matter how hard I tried, at best I was criticised, and at worst, rewarded with undiluted indifference. I remember once you told me that hate is not the opposite of love, indifference is. I understand that now. Thank you. 'The definition of insanity is doing the same thing over and over again and expecting different results.' I understand that now. I see now with a clarity that had previously eluded me. My parents are dead. One is dead to the world; I mourn him still with a grief that can never be healed. The other is dead to me.

Thanks for the lessons in independence. Being confronted with my bags packed at 16 made me grow up fast. But of course, I was expecting it. As each year passed, you told me how much closer you were to being free of me. So at least my expectations were well managed. I am resourceful. I work hard, I exceed expectations. I'm strong. I excel. I don't cry. I pull up my big girl pants, take a deep breath and get on with it. And I share none of that with you. My life is my life. I choose who belongs in it. Sadly, you didn't make the cut.

You told me once that blood is thicker than water, and that irrespective of my preference, I am part of the family. It turns out you were right, just not in the way you expected. The blood of the covenant is absolutely thicker than the water of the womb. The family I have created for myself far exceeds the one I was born into. And for that I am so blessed. The covenant I made for myself helped me to survive the hurt and anger that you gave me. And you are so resentful of that now. Now I'm a 'grown-up,' you need me now, in the same way I needed you then. It's too little too late. Of course I am bitter.

Of course I am my father's daughter. And of course I am done with you.

Let me tell you a secret. My children are the lucky ones. I am an exceptional mother. And I didn't learn that from you. Every time a situation presents itself, I wonder what you'd do and I do the opposite. Like I said, I'm blessed. I found a family that taught me compassion and understanding and love. I found a family I could call home. You think they stole me from you. Honestly, my feet carried me as fast and far away from your toxicity as they could. I was fortunate to find a sanctuary instead of a prison. I was fortunate to learn what love is and what it looks like.

So. I listen to my children. I play with them. I reassure them. I talk to them. I support them. I don't judge them. I don't persecute them. I am motivated by love and the certainty that they will never experience the pain that I did. I am their passionate protector. I have claws and teeth. The big bad wolf is scared of me. I don't protect them from the fire. I am the fire. And I would set the world alight to create a path for them. Maybe I'll tell you about that one day. More likely I won't. You can't possibly understand.

Jessica Arragon

LUNCH

It was a blistering hot day. The two men had been working since just before dawn. Their bodies were caked in sweat and dirt. Around them the yard was awash with activity. Their job was just one of many, completing brickwork for a wall in what would one day be a multi storey office building. At the moment it was barely one floor. It would take a lot of work. They had been at it for hours. Giving each other a fleeting glance, they downed tools. Work could do without them for ten minutes.

They made their way over to a secluded area of the yard. Ted, the younger of the two, produced a sandwich and a flask of coffee which he proceeded to offer to his colleague, his senior by ten years. Alfred nodded his thanks.

"It's good to get away," remarked Ted.

"Yes we're lucky if we can have five minutes rest these days," muttered Alfred.

It was true the company had been working them harder recently.

Ted sighed. "Still, we're lucky to have this job."

He knew it was true – neither of them could afford to be without work. Alfred's wife had lost her job that year and Ted knew that his friend was struggling. It wasn't fair. He wished things could be better, they both did.

Suddenly a voice interrupted their thoughts and shattered their moment of solace. "Who said you two could take a break?"

It was the foreman – a fat, red faced man clad in a pinstripe suit. He was looking at their tools and hopping up and down furiously. "Hurry up and finish," he bristled and stormed off, obviously not caring why they'd actually stopped.

Ted and Alfred looked at each other and both suppressed a laugh as the man walked away. Finally, Alfred turned to his friend and smiled.

"You know these jobs are all the same. Maybe the work varies but at end of the day, it's just another job."

Folk's Tales

Ted knew he was right. The work might be hard, the foreman might be a fool, but at least there was still time for a bit of lunch and friendship. Still laughing, they packed up their food and went back to work.

Ross Punton

MAYPOLE DANCERS

We leave at night, when the world bids farewell to the last of its light.
We start solemnly, two by two we go, carrying carefully our symbol, our tradition.
Marching along, we stop by a little mound of earth, delicately but firmly placing our gift.
The earth, as though waiting, welcomes it.
Our maypole.
We begin. Our cares, as we move, we leave behind.
We dance, we duck, we weave.
Round and round the mound we go.
Holding our flames like flowers of yellow light in the dark.
Round and round we dare not slow, lest the little people show.
We know they are there, in the mound, hiding just below ground.
Soon the Spring will be here.
It's coming, it's so near, we can feel it everywhere.
It's inside us, making us dance, making us cheer.
Old tales are unearthed, whilst new ones are given birth.
I know, years on, people may not know I was here.
I wonder, are there truly people under the mound?
If not, I wonder where they can be found?
I wonder, will my people's traditions last?
Or like me, will they come to pass?
Spring comes and goes for us all.
Right now, it matters not.
Right now, we dance, we join hands, circle our maypole again.
For a second, do I hear the little folk too?
We dance.

Ross Punton

WELCOME TO THE INTERDIMENSIONAL IMPOUND

Sigh. Another day.
Welcome to the interdimensional impound!
Listen everyone!!!
Not a sound.
I don't care, no one wants to be here.
You may all think you're big shots.
Think your status means some respect is owed.
Well not here my dear.
If you drive it, we can tow it.
Okay. Who's first?
Oh, it's you again. Yes I know who you are with your posh car.
I know you work at queen and country's behest.
I'm not impressed. You think you are above the law.
Pay your fine or you won't get your car.
Well, I'm sorry Mr Bond you shouldn't have spent so long chatting to the blonde.
Next.
Do you know what speed you were going at? Is that vehicle even registered?
Mr Skywalker, I don't care if it's in a galaxy far away, I need your paperwork by the end of the day. No, I will not give you the car, stop waving. I don't care what the force has to say.
Bloody hippies.
Next. Ah it's you, the worst of the bunch. No discipline at all. If I had my way, scum like you would have no license at all.
Don't give me those eyes.
Noddy your parking is shoddy.
You also hit three skittle men today. Noddy you pay or you're going away.
Yes, I know they're toys. Emotional damage they say.
What, Noddy, did you think your life was just play?

Sigh. On we go. Yes Mr Potter, leaving your broom where its parked will in fact be trouble. Glinda did you even check you were allowed to park that bubble?

Honestly, you people. You all think you have something special. Well all I can say…

Oh, it's after five.

All right everybody go away. I'm done for the day.

Please go away.

What a lot of over-rated rabble, that's all I can say.

Ross Punton

THE LEPRECHAUN'S LAMENT

Yes, I am a leprechaun.
Who are you, cap in hand?
You caught me, but I must say you've been misled.
There is nothing at the rainbow's end.
Yes, they are beautiful but watch them fade away.
You can't live on dreams at the end of a rainy day.
Crock of gold?
Let me set the record straight.
I don't have a bean.
Not one penny.
So don't be looking for a leprechaun to fix your fate.
Yes, let me set the record straight.
Look at me, take me in.
My shoes are worn, my clothes are ragged and torn.
I have no magic to grant a wish.
Why are you crying?
You think I should feel sorry for you?
I am the one to feel pity for!!!
Let me tell you the truth about my gold.
For years I saved every penny for when I was old.
Years ago, I thought I had the perfect place, yet I was found.
Whilst I slept, a thief was abroad.
Yet it gets worse.
Not only did some chancer Irish man steal every penny I had in my purse.
That man, on him, I wish a curse.
Even worse, since then, people have been coming to ask for more.
Beseeched for what I do not have.
Yes, I am the one to feel pity for.
Everyone wants money from me – I will be bothered for ever more.

Ross Punton

TIME MACHINES

The sixtieth pulse brings the fourth beat, after the twelfth stroke. The Folk Train growls away from Platform 6. Newcastle to Carlisle, a steady rock and roll along the Tyne Valley. From the outside, the Folk Train is an ordinary train, a Sprinter. Nearby Azumas are shaped to glide; Sprinters not so much, more stubborn. This Sunday's riders hint at difference; led by a green-banded top hat, there is a troupe with curved cases in hand. These are musicians, self-assembling in the middle of one carriage, interested passengers gathering around.

Countless once-upon-a-times ago, by daylight, by candlelight, by moonlight, individuals experimented. What might make monotony tick away quicker, leaven apathy, enliven fatigue. Yards, mills, barnyards. Surroundings cast in song. Emotions gathered. Memories broadcast into the air. Dialects and accents. Some worked solo, some duo-ed, some trio-ed, others in other beat combinations. Big John thought that he had a new tune. Micky turned a hymn earthward. Billy flashed his teeth, then his feet. Molly drew back her bow. A million hours, a thousand improvised elements alchemised, vibrations of floorboards, clacks of cobbles.

Christmas, Easter, May. Festivals. Receptions, wakes, weekends. The rising atmospheres of bars, lowering pressures, raising pulses. Those alchemies which reward are retained; others finessed, or discarded. Clogged feet clap, steeled heels clip. Breeches, blouses, shirts, braces nod, bow and jig and skip and reel in appreciation. Rinse off the sweat and repeat. No need to write it down (amongst those who could, or could be bothered)—memory and muscle memory would point these moments futureward. Pass it on to the future generations:

Come here, my little Jacky
Now I've smoked my baccy
Let's have a bit cracky
Till the boat comes in
Pass them on.

Folk's Tales

The top hat, atop the lean stately man, nods and bids welcome to the assembled congregation. The top hat then nods each improvised combination to order and time. Two, three, four! Time signatures are regular, keeping footstamps and hand claps easy.

New faces appear with regularity, every 5 to 10 minutes, peering from platforms outside at intermediate stations en route. They appear over the lower edges of the windows like bemused suburban next-doors, overlooking the tut-tut garden fence.

For a shortened hour, until Bardon Mill, the heirs of Big John pass on his tune. Micky's heirs recall his words. Molly's heirs draw back their bows, strum their strings, drum their bodhráns, ease their accordions, whistle flutes, flute whistles. Surroundings of a sometime somewhere recast in song. Memories recast into the air. Emotions regathered. Everyone else is Billy's heir, flashing hands in time with feet. Thousands of improvisations are distilled by these players into new alchemies, spells which bind friends and strangers alike. And they are chorused by, and provide a chorus to a fairytale, once-upon-a-time, sprinkling stardust magic—clogged feet clacking, steeled heels clipping. Breeches, blouses, shirts, braces nod and jig and skip and reel in appreciation. Conjure past into present, into the future, through memory, muscle memory, aural memory and oral memory. A white heavy horse gallops to the beat across its paddock. Jig, skip, reel in appreciation. Rinse off the sweat and repeat.

In Bardon Mill on Sunday. No special day today, except that the Folk Train has rolled in, a crowd has streamed out, up and over the footbridge, and has mainly strolled (with some keen exceptions) to the pub. Grab a pew, is this one taken? Shucks, must search for another. The regulars have their allotted spaces, bar stools against the bar top. The Folk Train folk mass around tables, mill at the bar, hubbubing this particular day's normalcy away. Thirsty work this playing, this listening, needs proper refreshment. Mine's a pint of me usual. Common on, pass it over here. As for food, this Cullen Skink tastes just like how my Highland Grandma used to cook it.

Folk's Tales

And after the consumption, to help the digestion, more music. A different set of tunes, perhaps a little more sedate than before, but maybe it is the different location. More drawing back of bows, strumming of strings, drumming of bodhráns, easing of accordions, whistling of flutes, fluting of whistles, flashing of hands and feet. Some in the audience exercising knee-high memories, chorusing with a hint of carousing as the afternoon rolls on.

On the train, rolling back. My eye is cornered to its right, my companion points her phone at me. I am momentarily frozen, in time, digital amber. I might be clapping, flashing my own hands, stamping my own feet. I too join in the hour, help to make the moment. More spells to be cast, atmospheres and elements alchemised, two, three, four! Keep the time regular. Hear the heirs sing and draw, pluck and strum, whistle and flute and drum. See the heirs nod, bow and jig and skip and reel. Flash, stamp, clip. Come over here. Pass it on.

Wayne Medford

THE MONOLITH

Nobody could stop the plans. DCMS had granted permission to build Ainsworth Towers, a luxury apartment complex. The land had been inspected and authorised via all available avenues. Even the local mayor, in his purely ceremonial role, approved. He had become one of the construction's greatest advocates.

Prior to the planning approval of the new housing blocks, the site was hogged solely by an ancient Pagan monolith, which sprouted from the ground, several hundred yards away from the local town. It was taller than three men stood foot-on-shoulder, and white smears trailed down its surface. The locals nicknamed it Nature's Tongue, its purpose unknown by archaeologists. Whether built for reasons of sacrifice, worship, or both, it was subject to schoolyard superstition and intoxicated yarns among the locals. In protest at the recent news, a white-robed crowd surrounded it like grapes on a stem. A journalist caught their demonstration on camera and immortalized it in the local paper, under the headline: *"WE'LL GIVE 'EM THE ROUGH EDGE OF OUR TONGUE" SAY LOCALS, UNDER CONTROVERSIAL PLANS TO BUILD LUXURY FLATS NEAR UNESCO-DESIGNATED MONOLITH.*

Mr Ed Ainsworth saw this in the paper, coffee in hand, seated at his dining table, wearing a luxury cream polo and joggers. Why did they care? This block of flats would not affect the surrounding area, nor would it hurt the sight of Nature's Tongue. He didn't take the protesters too seriously. After all, that crowd, frozen in photograph-form, were merely his emails and social media DMs made manifest. Bloody nimbyism, and people's preciousness about history. Things simply can't last forever. And as for UNESCO's warnings, like hell would he let some foreign bureaucrats boss him around. His father had faced similar squabbling.

His eyes on the paper, he heard his maid walk towards him. She was a middle-aged Indian woman named Navya, with bob hair, whose curtains she kept tied back. He hired her two weeks ago, after he ran into some trouble with her predecessor, who complained of financial irregularities. He heard Nayva's voice say: "Mr Ainsworth, I am done for today." It was almost five p.m., end of shift.

"Okay," he replied. He didn't look up and had now moved onto a story about commie kids with their gazillion genders.

"See you tomorrow," she said, half to herself. He heard the clomp of her clogs as she walked away, a rustle when she took her coat from the door hook, and the door clicking shut when she left.

He got up from his dining chair, towards the living area on the other side of the room, which opened onto wall-length windows looking out onto the lake ahead. He sat on the settee facing the window. The sun hung above the horizon, splintered across the sky, with an orange tail scattered along the surface of the water leading to the window. It looked like an erupted atom bomb.

On the ground floor, the modern white walls glowed in the sunshine, the furniture shades of brown, or black. Everything – kitchen, dining, living – was open plan except the toilet beneath the stairs.

He spent the next few hours watching TV, mounted onto the wall on the left of the living area. He stuck purely to streaming service content, avoiding the news channels.

Bedtime. Upon entering his bedroom, and seeing his empty bed, he was painfully hit with a desire to start dating again. It had been a long time. Too tired to shower, he just entered the ensuite bathroom and dropped his clothes in the basket, briefly catching his nude self in the mirror, muscular and bearded. He then slipped into pyjamas and crawled into bed. On his nightstand, two books stacked atop one another: a dog-eared copy of Sun Tzu's *The Art of War*, and the newly published *Top of the World: 30 Hacks for a Satisfying and Successful Leadership*, which came highly recommended by a friend. He read the first 50 pages before folding a corner on the next chapter, turning off his lamp, and dozing off.

Folk's Tales

He awoke in the darkness, briefly forgetting his surroundings. The first thing he saw was the vague outline of his ceiling above him. Lowering his head, at the foot of his bed, did he see an indiscernible white mass standing upright? No, surely, he was imagining things. He turned the lamp on. He saw what it was. A tsunami of chills waved across his entire body, and his bowels turned to water. It was a white-robed figure, scrunched over to the side, like it didn't know how to operate its own body. There was a shadow where its face should have been. Ainsworth tried to scream but could not. He lay stiff as the dead, his mouth desert dry.

"Ainsworth," it said, in a hybrid of fry and staccato, as if it hadn't spoken for years, and was internally taking note of mouth sounds as soon as it uttered them. "Leave be the land! Now! Or consequences will befall you!" The figure's arms then flattened, with a loud crunch. Then its legs. Crunch. Ainsworth's heart rattled in his chest like a caged, rabid, rottweiler. With the figure's limbs now crushed more easily than a bag of Doritos under a Doc Marten, it began to levitate. Then its hood lowered without limb assistance, revealing a black fog floating above its neck. The figure flew towards him -

Ed awoke in a cold sweat, screaming. He jumped out of bed. His room was unchanged, the furniture unmoved. The only new presence were the small specks of dust falling softly in the sunlight through the window, which shone squares of light on the floor. No footprints led from it, or the door. He was alone.

That morning, he checked the household CCTV. That thing may have been someone, after all, but they were playing a prank on him, taking advantage of the ambiguity of darkness. It might have been that maid of his. That frigid hag has always hated him. He considered firing her. However, a look at all the cameras revealed nothing. He had to concede his first suspicion, that he was overworked, and so engaged in a flight of fancy. But how did that thing feel so real? Did his brain make it up? Or take it from some movie he saw once? He surrendered his doubts to the unknown powers of the brain, but this did not allay his fears.

***

A week later, Ed's phone rang. It was James, his assistant.
"Hello?" Ed asked, sitting on his settee.
"Ed."
"What's up, mate?"
"You seen the news this morning?"
"What news?"
The mayor, dead in his bed, in mysterious circumstances. Investigators concluded a heart attack took him, strange for healthy man in his mid-thirties. His eyes and mouth were wide open, as if he was mid-scream, his skin snow white.

Ed had a lump in his throat, "You're - you're - having me on, right?"
"Well, no. Sorry to tell you".

Ed's stomach churned as he remembered last week's events. He felt insane. Were these the consequences? Already, the room's walls seemed to clamp towards him like the inside of an iron maiden.

"D - do they suspect foul play?"
"Don't see how. Heart attack's a pretty natural thing, and his wife was in bed with him at the time. Apparently, he just screamed in his sleep, then… that was it. Horrible way to go."

A few seconds of silence.

"Sorry, it's a lot to take in," James continued.
"Yeah, yeah. It is. It is a horrible way to go. Christ. Anyway, I gotta go," Ed said, before exiting the call. What was going on? Could he cancel now? He felt mad for believing the events in his bedroom last week were real, but what other explanations were there? He scanned his bedroom again. He had tears in his eyes, and swallowed, and, to no-one, said: "Okay, okay. You win. Y - you win, okay?" He didn't know if he'd get an answer, but he wanted to speak his mind just in case. "Gimme a minute. Just a minute. A… another week. That's all I ask."

Folk's Tales

***

Ainsworth cancelled Ainsworth Towers. His cited reasons? Pressure from UNESCO and the impassioned local protests. Some townspeople thought that strange. Mr Ainsworth was so adamant about building these towers. After all, it's what the mayor would have wanted. When the press followed up on these matters, he responded – eyes distant and beard unkempt – by saying that he was a very open-minded man. Several months later, a scandal about his employment practices was leaked to the tabloids.

Today, Nature's Tongue stands like a nail holding down the earth. It faces the town whose birth it witnessed and is visited by tourists it has outlived generations of. Modern constructions have not since touched its ground.

Joss Hancock

BANDSTAND

On my walk through the wintery park
I come to the empty bandstand
Inside my footsteps echo
my feet rediscovering
the beautiful notes of the summer tunes we played
on the cheerful fiddle
the soulful flute
the mellow guitar
The ones that didn't drift away on the wind
the ones that fell to the floor
and still live there

I take off my gloves and pick one up
It's warm

                                                    Renata Connors

LET ME TELL YOU ABOUT THE HEDLEY KOW

First, it's not a cow, not really. It's generally described as a sort of goblin or bogle-type creature, although some depictions include some cow-like features, I suppose just to be on the safe side.

The Kow lives in rural Northumberland, can change its shape at will and seems to spend most of its time using this ability to play tricks on people. The tricks are pretty lowbrow – stuff like turning into a cow and causing chaos at milking time or taking the form of young fellers' sweethearts and running away, luring them into bogs. You get the idea: annoying but not too malign, tolerated grudgingly by the local populace. I don't know anything about its living arrangements or there being any other creatures of the same ilk around. It presumably lives by itself in the woods when not out causing mild trouble.

One tale of the Hedley Kow concerns the Kow's continuing attempts to trick an old woman.

The Kow's begins its scheme by transforming into a large pot and depositing itself on a forest road. This is where the old woman finds it. She is not well-off, living alone and scratching a meagre subsistence through a range of countryside drudgery. Naturally, then, after finding no pot-owners in the vicinity, she decides to drag this unexpected find home.

After travelling a little way, the Kow progresses its subterfuge by transforming so that the pot is now filled with gold coins. The old woman eventually notices and is amazed and delighted. How could she have missed this? What incredible luck!

She continues to drag the pot homeward. The next time she takes a breather and checks on the contents of the pot, the Kow has changed again – now, the pot is filled with silver. Whilst this is worth rather less than the gold, the woman notes aloud that she must have been mistaken about the gold, but this will be simpler to sell and will still be a tremendous windfall. She remains delighted.

A little further along the road, the old woman has another rest and check on the mysterious pot; she discovers it now seems to be filled with iron, rather than silver. Is she dismayed? No! She says to herself that iron is even easier to sell than the silver and will still be worth some coin – not bad for something found in the road.

Once she reaches her home, the Kow pulls one more alteration and becomes, simply, a rock. This is undeniably less of a prize than a pot (of gold or otherwise). However, the old woman remains indefatigably cheery. She remarks how useful the rock will be to prop her door open in the summer.

At this, the Kow takes on its true, possibly-cow-like, goblin-ish form and shouts something along the lines of, "Surprise! It's me – the Hedley Kow!"

The old woman, with entirely nothing to show for her endeavours, is, if anything, cheerier than ever. She says how incredible it is to have met the infamous Hedley Kow and what a good anecdote this will make.

What happens at this point is slightly unclear, but she possibly invites the Kow in for some dinner, and it possibly accepts, having delivered a satisfactory pranking.

After dinner, the Kow possibly provides some small quantity of actual treasure in acknowledgement of the old woman taking the pranking in such good spirits.

Superficially, the message of trying to see the positive in any situation is pleasing. Keeping upbeat in the face of all of life's indignities is very much something to aspire to.

However, what gets me is this: we are all aware of our own capacity to be mistaken, but the sequence of changes (empty to gold to silver to iron to just a rock) is so radical that it seems utterly implausible that the old woman could not realise that some supernatural trickery was afoot. Particularly in the context of there being a well-reported creature capable of such phenomena in the area, her reactions are hard to take at face value.

Folk's Tales

One interpretation could be that, suspecting it was the Kow, she may have felt there was a chance that if she played along, she might still eventually get some reward. Given the Kow's highly erratic nature, that seems a long shot, hardly worth the investment of effort.

I think she would have heard plenty of stories about the peculiar cow-goblin fooling about the countryside, attempting underwhelming tricks on people, scarpering off on its own. I wonder if she thought that it might be lonely. Maybe she thought it might like some dinner and a break from all the antics and the running away and the being on its own.

Maybe she herself might have welcomed the company too, even such company as this.

I think this is the best interpretation.

I try and picture its goofy cow-goblin face, as it sits eating dinner with her. I think it would be the first dinner it had been given in a long while. I wonder about whether it would realise that the woman was humouring it, providing dinner not out of deference but out of sympathy. In my head, I think it does realise that, but it doesn't know how to respond, other than just to go in and have the dinner, because it has been such a long time since anyone has given it some dinner (even though actually maybe it quite likes dinner). I picture them having a little chat, and the Kow trying its best to remember how to have a normal conversation. I think they talk a little about the nearby villages and she encourages it to eats healthily and look after itself, and she says if it ever feels like a break from all the pranks and the running away, it can come back and have some more dinner.

And I hope it does.

Alexi Calamity

NOT ENTIRELY A HERO

Tim was average, or at least so he thought. Average height, weight, brown hair and eyes. His school reports that had been presented to his parents were average. He lived in an average rented house with his sister and parents. There was nothing different at all and he certainly wasn't a hero, unlike his dad. His dad had fought Germans in the war.

Today also looked average to him, a bit cloudy but not too hot or cold. He walked to school the same route he always took, past the off-licence and the town's main store. Then he noticed his shoe was loose. He crouched down and started to tie the lace.

He could hear a woman shouting, and running. A man raced around the corner straight into him. Crouched down he couldn't move out of the way in time so took the impact of his legs on his side. The man fell over and hit his head on a lamp post, dropping something.

Tim grabbed the purse as it fell right in front of his face. A woman appeared, screaming "Thief!"

Thinking quickly Tim proffered the purse, "This yours?"

"Yeah," the woman snatched it from him. "That thief stole it from me. Sorry but there are some important things in here, not that he could use them."

A security guard came out of the store and detained the thief, and another man with some kind of camera. He talked to the woman, and took Tim's name.

Tim explained he needed to go to school, it was nearly nine.

Arbuck Comprehensive was an average school suitable for an average town. Assembly over quickly, Tim went off for his first class. His side still hurt a bit where the thief had hit him but it didn't seem bad, not enough to go and see the nurse for. Two periods of mathematics, something he was average at, but he liked it.

Folk's Tales

Then break and Miss Trenchard came and said to follow her. He didn't ask why, just wondered if he was in trouble. She led him straight to the headmaster's room.

At least Mister Cuthbert didn't look displeased. "So here is the little hero?"

Tim wondered if the head had gone wrong in the head, "Who?"

"You stopping that thief before getting into school," Mister Cuthbert stated. "It's been on the radio not ten minutes ago. You will have to talk to the police, but with one of your parents present. If everything goes well, we will announce what you did tomorrow morning in assembly."

Tim felt rather shell shocked and a bit awed. The fact was he hadn't done anything much but should he say so? "I, umm, don't feel like a hero. My side still hurts a bit."

The headmaster looked at him, "Next you go and see the nurse, get it looked at. Not checking injuries can be a problem. Can you take him, Miss Trenchard?"

That evening Tim's mum sat with him while one of the local news reporters filmed an interview for TV. He didn't actually say much but his mum made up for that, slightly embellishing the earlier interview with the woman that had been put out earlier. He had been willing to tell the truth but getting anything past his mum was near impossible, so he just sat there and smiled.

His dad was working away so he couldn't talk to him, and his sister was having another 'locked in her room time' after a row with her boyfriend.

The next day he went to school as normal. The headmaster pulled him out and told the other children what had been reported. How he had single-handedly managed to take down an adult thief and recover the stolen purse. Most of it wasn't true but he was embarrassed, and even trying to correct the headmaster just felt wrong too. The other children cheered and clapped for him, which just made him feel a little worse.

The dinner lady seemed to recognise him too, and put extra food on his plate. All he really wanted was for people to forget about it and for everything be normal again. He didn't feel a hero, or believe he really was one. His dad had climbed up to a German position while under fire and threw grenades into it, and shot the Germans. His dad was a real hero. Although only his mother talked about it and he was fairly sure she had added to it a bit. There probably hadn't been twenty Germans.

With school out Tim went home. His dad was sitting on the settee, apparently arrived back early. "So how is being a hero shaping up son?"

"I don't feel like a hero," Tim admitted unhappily. "The woman didn't see what happened, just got there for me to give her the purse back. I was doing up my shoelace when the man fell over me. I feel like I'm a fake."

"Well, admitting that is a big move for anyone," his father said. "And since you've admitted it, I think I should admit things too. Make it even. When the Germans opened up with their machine gun I was away from the other men, having a pee. They were pinned down, unable to move so I did climb the hill with four grenades and a Thompson submachine gun. I wasn't frightened, I was angry at them shooting. I got almost to the point where I could throw the grenades in and then…"

His dad paused for a good few seconds. "A mortar shell fell right into their position. The gun was silenced already but, as I'd pulled the pin from the first grenade, I threw it in anyway. Then I crept up to the edge and looked in. There was three dead Jerries in there, their machine gun smashed. Inevitably they were dead before I had thrown the Mills bomb. Anyway, my platoon came up and saw where I was. They assumed I had done it. Well, I nearly had. I got a medal for it, and a report was published in the local paper."

"So, what mum has been saying isn't true either?"

"I don't think that matters. You see, it's not always what really happened that matters, as long as everything sorts itself out. I went on to do a lot more than grenade three dead Germans, but that's the one what your mum always remembers. I have four other medals for bravery. Should have been a couple more but those wasn't reported back, that made up for the one that I got initially. By Monday the whole thing will probably be forgotten, except by your mum."

Tim looked at his father, "you mean?"

"You might not be the bravest hero but, accidentally or not, you did make a difference. From now on, in whatever you do, you have a chance to make up for the credit."

Tim smiled, "Thanks dad."

"What for?"

"For being you, a hero."

Arthur J. Montieth

FOLK SHOULD NOT BRING SPIRITS

The timewasters eventually departed. House selling was horrendous.
'The spirits like your family.'
What sort of idiot says that on your landing?
Bridget, now calmer, cuddles Ella.
'Mummy, my new friend is here.'
Bridget's blood curdles: the rocking chair is unoccupied and moving violently.
'It's Irene, Mummy, she isn't very happy, she likes our family and wants us to stay.'

Alison Sidney

NO WEDDING AND A FUNERAL

Mum was very supportive when I got jilted at the altar. Folk had come from several counties to inadvertently witness the most excruciating day of my life.

"Sorry I haven't got time..." had literally been Giles' explanation. Apparently, his merger came first. What he omitted to mention was that it was a merger with my bridesmaid, and former best friend Charlotte and she was pregnant with their child.

Thankfully Mum, ever the planner, had taken out wedding insurance. She had never liked Giles, and we had a holiday in Florence to recover with some of the insurance money.

Fast forward several years and I found something much more up my proverbial street. Funerals. You didn't get jilted at your funeral. Mum had attended them secretly for years and I got the bug. I have always looked rather good in black. I now have a selection of outfits for funerals, and we try to attend at least one a week. I like the camaraderie of the event and the deceased always turn up. It also makes me feel close to poor, departed Dad.

Mum explained that you must study the deceased in some detail. The obituaries help but funeral entry is so much harder these days; the posher ones are invitation only. So, Mum suggested we concentrate on the next town, explaining that the buffets have improved, and she can do some of the leg work for me (not literally, as she has severe arthritis in her knees). At this point it is pertinent to explain that we avoid children's funerals and suicides as a mark of respect. Hard core grieving is not our forte.

Anyway, I digress. Millicent Spencer, my former teacher, was our latest coup. Ninety, and thrilling because I had known her. I hadn't liked her. She'd had a tongue like a razor and delighted in shredding me with it for my inability to read (dyslexia wasn't recognised then). Stating that I could just get married instead. It would appear she wasn't clairvoyant.

It was to be a burial. What fun, and rather unusual for November due to the vagaries of the British weather. I had decided on my Victorian ensemble, heavy silk dress, lace up boots and my cashmere coat from the Cancer Research Shop. Mum had her black wool coat with real fur collar. I was rather worried that she would get cold in her wheelchair, but she refused to wear trousers (bad form at funerals), so I purloined a nice Stewart tartan blanket from the same shop when the assistant wasn't looking.

The order of service was pedestrian and the hymns uninspiring. They excelled with the floral tributes though, and I obtained several photos for our album and the little biography pamphlet of the old bat.

After the service we spot a fellow funeral afficionado, Mrs Castille. Since Godfrey passed she doesn't get to many funerals as she doesn't drive, but I am pleased to be able to offer her a lift to the buffet. It is quite fortuitous as she is fitter than Mum. So, when I succumb to this cancer, Mum will have company. The medics have given me several months. Plenty of time to organise a taxi account for them both, and plan my dream funeral.

Alison Sidney

DON'T TALK TO STRANGERS

Right everyone, please take your seats so we can get started... come along now. Goldilocks, if you could kindly wait until after the meeting before you start dishing out the porridge, that would be much appreciated.

I knew it was a mistake inviting her to join the group. Just because she gets her name in the title of her story, she thinks she's a cut above the rest of us.

Okay, now you're sitting comfortably, I'll begin. I'm sure everyone knows me but, for any newcomers, allow me to introduce myself. I am Maleficent – of Sleeping Beauty fame – and, as this year's President, it is my absolute pleasure to welcome you to October's CON meeting. I have one apology from The Pied Piper. The babysitter cancelled at the last minute, so he needs to stay home and look after the children. However, he asked me to pass on his best wishes and looks forward to seeing us all next time.

The fool clearly didn't realise what he was letting himself in for, adopting all those awful brats. He really has no idea about discipline whatsoever, the little tykes run rings around him.

Now, as you know, we set up the Clear Our Names support group two years ago, to try and combat the negative press we so-called 'bad guys' have had to put up with for years. Yes, Goldilocks, I appreciate that at least half of us are girls and not guys, but I'm afraid that's the term we've been given by the media, so that's what we're dealing with, whether we like it or not.

You don't always get what you deserve in this life, let me tell you, young lady.

Speaking of the media, if you've read the briefing notes I circulated prior to the meeting, you'll be aware that I've managed to pull off something of a coup, if I do say so myself. After an awful lot of phone calls, I've finally found a journalist who's prepared to interview one of us and let us see the draft before it goes to print. Yes, thank you for your helpful comments, Shere Khan. I realise that the 'Woodland Weekly' doesn't exactly give us national coverage, but it's a start, isn't it?

Suddenly, everyone's an expert. I know just how The Little Red Hen felt. No-one wants to help with the work, but they all want a share of the glory.

If we could return to the matter at hand, please. I'm sure we're all keen to avoid a repeat of last year's PigGate catastrophe, aren't we? Those scandal-mongering Grimm Brothers have got a lot to answer for. Anyway, a young journalist named Mr Andersen has agreed to tell the world the true story of those tearaways, Hansel and Gretel. It's time people saw behind this façade of two innocent little children, just out for a walk in the woods.

How they got away without a custodial sentence after they broke into Granny Betty's home, I'll never know. It took the poor woman months to rebuild her cottage after they'd eaten the roof and half the kitchen. If she hadn't managed to raise the alarm, they would have started on the bedroom as well. The whole incident was quite disgraceful.

I understand that Elizabeth will be discharged from the clinic shortly and we'll be organising a rota to help with her shopping once she's back home. The Wicked Witch will be coming round with a clipboard, so just put a nice clear tick next to your name if you'd like to help. It's important that you put a tick please, and not a cross – it got very confusing last month when I was trying to work out who was free to take Captain Hook to his crocodile aversion therapy sessions.

What's that, Stepmother? Yes, that would be very helpful indeed if you could write everything down for the Troll. All that clip clopping back and forth over his bridge has made him quite deaf, the poor thing. I'm sure he misses half of the announcements. Now, where was I?

Ah yes… this Hans Christian chap has promised to listen to Betty and write a fair account of her side of the incident. More to the point, he's going to let us read it before it goes to print, so there shouldn't be any nasty surprises!

Frankly I'm not sure how much sense he'll get out of her. She's refused to eat anything but breadcrumbs for weeks now and keeps rambling on about tasty little children. She's clearly still traumatised. I do hope I don't live to regret this, it could seriously jeopardise my hopes of retaining the presidency next year.

Well, that concludes the business side of things for tonight, so it's time for refreshments. May I take this opportunity to thank Goldilocks for providing this month's food – hopefully everyone will find something that's 'just right' for them. Next month, Fox has kindly offered to bring some of his delicious gingerbread men for us to enjoy, so we look forward to that. He tells me he's been working on perfecting his icing techniques, so I'm sure we can expect great things.

Don't forget that Rumpelstiltskin will be selling the raffle tickets tonight and we have two excellent prizes up for grabs. Wolf has donated a lovely set of thermal underwear, a most welcome prize I'm sure, now the cold weather's setting in. He found a whole stack of them in Grandma's abandoned cottage and very thoughtfully brought along three different sets, so the winner can pick their favourite.

Tonight's second prize is a copy of the manual that's topped the Forest Folk Book List for the past three months now, Coping with Anxiety, written by our very own Cruella de Vil. It contains lots of simple, but extremely effective, exercises that can make a real difference to your mental health and wellbeing.

I could do with reading that myself, come to think of it. Trying to organise this lot is like herding cats. I know I make it look easy, but people have no idea how stressful being President really is. It took two boxes of dye to cover the grey hairs last time. Maybe I should speak to the hairdresser about changing this middle parting. A fringe might be better at hiding the wrinkles…

All the proceeds from this month's raffle will go to help Wolf's cousin, The Big Bad Wolf, who's currently facing a hefty bill for legal fees. His solicitors tell me he stands a good chance of winning his claim against the building firm as they were clearly negligent. If they'd done a proper job in the first place, there would have been no need for our friend to have climbed up on to the roof and try and repoint the Three Little Pigs' chimney for them. The injuries he sustained when he fell down the chimney and landed in the curry the pigs were

Folk's Tales

cooking on the fire were truly horrific. However, you'll be delighted to hear that Wolfie is now out of intensive care. He's back on the main ward and just waiting for a date for his fur grafts. Hopefully it won't be long before he's able to sit down without the aid of a rubber ring. We'll be arranging some hospital visits for later this week for anyone who'd like to go and see him.

Honestly what was he thinking? He's such a soft touch. Those little pigs should be ashamed of themselves, blatantly taking advantage of an elderly wolf. I'll be having words with their mother.

So, enjoy your porridge, buy some raffle tickets, and catch up with old friends. Please remember that we need to leave the hall in the same state we found it, so wash your mugs thoroughly and put all rubbish in the appropriate recycling bins before you leave. If you could stack the chairs and line them up at the side of the hall that would be most helpful. Remember to bend your knees when you lift though and, whatever you do, please don't try and carry more than two chairs at once.

Seriously, I don't think I could cope if anyone else ended up in hospital. These visiting rotas are driving me crazy. I thought I'd be spending this year mixing with Fairy Tale royalty and drinking elderflower champagne. Instead of which, here I am having to mix with the hoi polloi and eating some jumped-up girl's lumpy excuse for breakfast. Deep breaths, Maleficent, deep breaths.

Now, all that remains is for me to thank you for coming and to wish you a safe journey home. Take care when walking back through the forest, as Shere Khan would say – 'it's a jungle out there!' Stick to the paths… and don't talk to strangers!

Right, where did I put that hip flask…

Bridget Gallagher

LOST TREASURES

Icy hands pick over bone-like remains.
Common whelk carved by Poseidon into a dolphin
Shell breakfast abandoned along salty shore line
Trefoil footprints the only sign of oystercatchers running

Common whelk carved by Poseidon into a dolphin
Waves hiss and fizz, permeating unruffled sand
Trefoil footprints the only sign of oystercatchers running
Limpets guard the coal seam like miners' lamps

Waves hiss and fizz, permeating unruffled sand
Smallest specks of sea glass shine, opalescent
Limpets guard the coal seam like miners' lamps
Scallop shell, lunch of the gulls, washed clean

Smallest specks of sea glass shine, opalescent
Shell breakfast abandoned along salty shore line
Scallop shell, lunch of the gulls, washed clean
Icy hands pick over bone-like remains.

Jenny Smith

FROM CULLERCOATS TO NORTH SHIELDS – FOLLOWING THE HERRING

It was familiar women's work, this. So often as he had grown up, he had seen his mother, the fishwife. After Black Friday, she had made him promise not to take to the boats, the only one of her menfolk to survive. Yet the sea, the fishing, it called to him. He had travelled with the herring, south, honing his art and telling tales of the waves. Now he was seeking a new beginning.

He watched as they bent over the farlins. Their hands were made old by the knives, the salt, and the slippery fish, but their faces were fresh and young. Hair flattened under scarves, and aprons made of thick oil cloth covered their clothes. The darker haired girl had her sleeves rolled up, and her movements were economic and efficient.

He was drawn to her vibrancy. Her colour and vivacity stood out to him. He wanted to paint her. This was his skill. He took out a small book he kept concealed about his person for such reason and began to draw.

The lasses were strong. Vigorous. Hardly phased by the salt that caked the pans and the fish, the creels, their fingers, and the floor. They were synchronised, one gutting and sorting the spents from the matties while the others filled the rousing tub and stirred the brine. The fish rosettes were separated by thick layers of salt which they spread over with their bare hands. He noticed some of the women had wound strips of cloth around their fingers, worn through here and there. Barely realising what he was doing, he perched himself on a wide mooring post, fixing these small details on the page. Swift strokes of his pen made the young girl a proud beauty, lithe sun browned skin beside the folds of her cotton sleeves.

The girl worked on, eager to set each fish in its place and fill the barrel. Silver darlings were time as well as money. Each barrel meant more in her pocket, more for the family, enough for winter stockings to keep out the cold as she stood, packing tight the fish. She had grown up on the sand, scaling the rocks for limpets, bait for the lines, and setting and mending the nets. When the trawlers had started coming, the cobles had turned to the redfish for their catch, and she had followed the herring, down the Tyne and inland to the fish quay on the shields.

Her sister had walked with her and was long gone. Creel stuffed with fresh catch, she had taken her wares to hawk inland. They would both return home with money in their pockets, paid by the piece. The money brought its own freedoms. There was no need to tie the knot to any of the village fisher lads just yet.

It was not long before he drew their notice. Head buried in his book, he was unaware of the glances they exchanged and the sly nudges and smirks passing over his head. He was not the first and he would not be the last to immortalise certain of them in oil paint on canvas. They would not have heard, as he had, of the fisher lasses' labours made famous across the continent and the new world.

"Excuse me, sir? This is a workin' quay. Please mind your step."

She heard the gentle humour in the cooper's tone. He had seen many a curious gent come a cropper as they navigated the fish market, discovering how the other side lived, sliding on cobbles made slippery by brine and fish guts. Many came to photograph or sketch, or write in their notebooks about the herring girls. Some women tried their luck with the gutting or packing, but did not last. They did not have the stout boots and toughened hands for the job.

Brine slopped out of the farlins and onto the floor, and the stench coated the bandages on her hands. She must reek to high heaven, she realised, and a sudden blush covered her cheeks. Nellie, a Scot who was not known for her subtlety, poked her in the ribs, and muttered, "Aye, he's a bonnie lad," which heaped coals on the burning fire. The other girls around her sniggered, and she took her time cleaning the darlings, until she had composed herself enough to ignore them.

Folk's Tales

He was, she had to admit, handsome. His hat was pushed back, rakish, on his head, and his sleeves were rolled up, revealing tanned brown arms. He was an outsider, but she could feel a familiarity about him, a sharpness of the eye and deftness of hand that reminded her of her father, pulling in the catch. Closing his book, he looked at her for a moment, before jumping up from the post and walking away, his deliberate movements unnerving her. Even more unnerving was the sudden urge she had to run after him, to ask when she would see him again. If she would see him again.

There were slim pickings now in the trough, and the final barrels were being packed. Soon she would set off back to Cullercoats. She would help set the nets once she was home, and the chief responsibility of the cleaning and sweeping would fall to her also.

The resident girls were making their way back to their lodgings, up the steps and into town in twos and threes, arm in arm. Nellie, her gutting partner, had told her how they sat together and talked, those amongst them with sweethearts knitting them ganseys, or knitting for their families. In her own kist, Nellie had a board for chess, carefully worked by her father, and she and another buckie girl would sit together, smoking their pipes, and trade turns. She watched them, envying for a moment their freedom, and wondering if next year, she might follow the herring south, as the summer fishing carried on further down the coast. It had been accidental, her hiring. She and her sisters had come to fill the creel to sell. Among the herring girls there had been a shortage, and they were recruiting local fish lasses to fill the gap. She'd taken the cure, a pound, and taken home a precious wage to support the family through autumn. The work was hard, and her back ached from leaning over the trough. Her fingers sore where the cutag had caught them, and salt stung in the wounds. She was young, though, and quick at gutting, accurate and one of the swiftest, the fish flying over her shoulders and making the packing easy for Rosie.

Bait box and apron stowed in her creel, she wrapped her shawl around her shoulders in style of her village, and was about to set out the hour's walk for home when she saw him, moving towards her.

"Miss?"

A few of the girls still lingered, nudging each other as he spoke. She felt herself blush.

"Sir? My name is Dolly. You don't need to call me that."

She started to curtsey, but he held his hand out to stop her.

"Miss. Dolly. Please. You don't need to do that. I just wanted to give you this."

In his other hand he held something. Paper. She realised it was his sketch. Reaching out a hand before she could stop herself, she took it from him. Turned it. Saw herself through his eyes. No lingering odour or cuts from the gutting. Hard working, strong, a small link in a greater chain. She examined it, tracing the lines with her careful fingers.

"Thank you." She held it out to him.

He brushed her away, suddenly gruff. "I should thank you."

Safely pocketing the drawing, and shouldering the creel, she gestured to the coastal path. "I must go home. They will need me there before dark."

Silent, he moved in step beside her. She did not look his way, but her heart sang with the knowledge that he had not bid her good evening. Perhaps it showed on her face, for, in a moment, he asked her if she would follow the herring next year.

And she knew, just as surely, that if he asked her again, she would not.

Jenny Smith

OUTFOXED

"You should never trust a fox."
"Because they are notoriously tricky creatures."
"But this is something that I did not learn until recently."
On a moonlit night, a guy walks across a stretch of wasteland which is a shortcut as he makes his way home after a few post-work drinks.
Tyler (a thirty-three year old guy who is merry and maybe a little tipsy) tightly holds an unopened family sized bucket of fried chicken that he is saving until he gets home.
As he walks down this dimly lit path, he does not notice a pair of glowing yellow eyes that are watching him from the darkness.
Unable to resist his midnight feast any longer, Tyler opens up the bucket and he sniffs at the unmistakable smell of fried deliciousness which makes him salivate and he helps himself to a single leg of crispy chicken.
But he is not alone as Something in the Shadows smells and salivates too.
Tyler takes his first bite from the chicken leg. He savours the still warm and juicy chicken and the crispy crunchy coating.
Now, The Creature from the Darkness decides to make its move.
Emerging from the shadows, The Creature bounds out onto The Path in-front of Tyler and under the lights, it is revealed to be a Small Red Fox.
Tyler stops to look at The Fox and in return, The Fox looks at Tyler.
Surprised by this late-night up-close sighting of The Fox, Tyler takes the chicken leg out of his mouth, chews, and then swallows before remarking "Holy crap… it's a fox!".
"Holy crap… it's a human!" remarks The Fox.
Tyler is perplexed by The Vociferous Vulpine as it takes a moment for him to recover enough to ask The Fox "You can talk?"

"Yes."

"So, I'm not just imagining this?"

"Maybe… do you often imagine animals talking to you?"

Tyler thinks about this as he doesn't believe that he is insane or that he is a Disney Princess. He takes a second bite of the chicken leg and then answers "No"

Then he asks "Since when have foxes been able to talk?"

The Fox replies "Since always."

He goes to take the last bite of meat from the bone and chews on the mouthful as The Fox watches on. Its yellow eyes are almost envious of the man.

Tyler asks "Then why haven't I heard one talk before tonight?"

The Fox answers "You hunt us for sport… why would we talk to the hunters?"

Tyler points at The Fox with the bone and muses "That's a good point." but as he moves the leg, he notices that its attention is on the chicken leg in his right hand.

He asks "You want this?"

Tyler tosses the leg bone to The Fox.

The Fox catches the bone in mid-air.

When it lands, The Fox crunches the bone in two bites with a crackle and a snap.

The Fox licks its snout as it says "Thank you for your kindly donation…"

More Yellow Eyes appear in the darkness as The Fox continues "…but my friends are also hungry."

Tyler notices The Glowing Eyes and The Shapes Moving in the Darkness around him and he wonders if he is what is next on the menu.

Tyler slowly places the bucket of fried chicken down on the path, then he looks to The Fox and he says "It's all yours."

The Fox's eyes are fixed upon Tyler.

Nervously, he asks "Can I go?"

The Fox's eyes dart from The Human to the bucket of chicken and back again as if it is contemplating something, before saying "You may go."

Quickly, Tyler makes his way past The Fox and down the rest of the dimly lit path.

Behind him, The Fox and his friends descend upon the much easier prey of the bucket of fried chicken and the mewling and screeching sound of foxes fighting fills the air.

Tyler catches his breath as he stands on the well-lit street corner which is a few feet from the end of the path and he has had quite a weird evening after having a few words with the local wildlife but it's not quite over…

…as he hears The Fox call out to him "Human."

Tyler turns to see The Fox sitting at the end of the path with A Small Fabric Drawstring Bag in its mouth and it puts The Little Bag on the ground.

"You gave something to us… we must give you something in return."

It pushes forward with its nose to Tyler and it says "This is an ancient charm."

The Fox promises that "It will bring you good luck…"

Tyler walks over, picks up and accepts The Charm.

It also warns "…but you must never open the bag."

Bemused by this strange gift from the even stranger Fox, Tyler just says "Thanks?"

Looking back up from The Charm to the path, where there is no Fox or his kin and no bucket of chicken, Tyler decides that it would be best to call it a night and just go home.

Early the next morning, Tyler sprints down the street for the bus which is already at The Bus Stop.

As the tail lights of the bus begin to flash, in mere moments the bus will drive off.

He speeds up and Tyler reaches The Bus Stop… but the bus begins to pull away.

He jumps and he manages to get on board the bus before the doors close.

Tyler smiles like he's pulled off an Indiana Jones style stunt.

"Jumping on a moving bus is one thing…"

But The Bus Driver is not-at-all impressed.

"…but how lucky is this charm?"

Folk's Tales

Tyler smirks, flashes his bus pass and The Driver motions for him to take a seat.

In a busy office, Tyler sits at his desk with The Fox's Charm out on his desk. He looks at The Small Drawstring Bag and he wonders "How would I go about testing my luck?"

He looks up and across The Office to see Deborah, The Boss's Secretary at her desk. She is in her mid-twenties, a serious looking brunette with a slight gothic flavour to her. Think April from Parks and Rec.

Even though she is out of his league, he ponders; should I hit on Deborah?

Tyler gets up from his desk, walks over to The Boss's Secretary to test his luck. A few words are exchanged between the co-workers and Deborah smiles.

"Maybe it is my lucky day!"

Getting a little cocky, Tyler pushes his luck as he says one more thing which she doesn't quite appreciate and she slaps him.

The slap shakes Tyler out of his fantasy and back at his desk, he thinks to himself; perhaps I should try something that won't get me in trouble with HR.

Tyler is out of the office and out for lunch. He walks into a local convenience store.

"Last week, I would have said that luck is the stuff of superstitions and folktales."

Inside the small store, several people peruse the chillers of the meal deal aisle.

"But last night, I had a conversation with a talking fox."

After grabbing a ham and cheese roll, a bottle of flavoured water and some ready salted crisps, he heads to The Till.

"People believe in lucky numbers, lucky symbols and lucky charms."

At The Till, he notices The Lottery Stand advertising Tonight's Jackpot as a huge life changing amount of money. Believing that luck is on his side, he purchases a ticket.

"But they forget that The Rabbit's Foot is rarely lucky for the rabbit."

Tyler imagining what he will do with those millions of pounds, he smiles.

At home, Tyler watches TV as he excitedly waits for his numbers to come up.

"Sometimes you have good luck."

The six winning numbers are revealed…

"Sometimes you have bad luck."

…and they are all one number off the ones that Tyler chose.

Annoyed, Tyler crumples up his ticket, he decides to see what is inside The Charm by opening up the drawstring bag and a look of absolute disgust crosses Tyler's face.

"And sometimes your luck just turns to shit."

Turns out that The Ancient Charm is just A Fossilised Fox Turd.

                                                  Chris Longstaff

MISS JONES

She is in her 70th year,
An elegance radiates from her tired eyes.
If you look closely, you can see the twinkle of youthfulness that has not
been totally lost. Her hair has a tinge of strawberry blonde which
complements her pale features.

Little does anyone know about her life before; if they had known, they might have
stopped to find out more.
She has never married or had children, she is content in knowing that her life
has taken her in a different direction.

Her job is nothing short of fascinating. She still has a sharp sense of summing
others up, and has no restraint when others ask her opinion.
As she sits, staring out the window, in the Orange Tree coffee shop,
Finishing off her vanilla slice and latte, she plans her next move.

She stands up and grabs her shopping trolley.
Just a 70-year-old woman on her daily business. However, in her trolley sits a
Ruger 22. For Mavis Jones is no ordinary woman: she is a hired assassin and
she has more plans for her day. It seems that we never can tell what secrets
some folk hide. As the saying goes,

'There is nowt queerer than folk.'

Pureheart Wolf

Folk's Tales

HOME IS WHERE THE FOLK RESIDE

Picture a seaside town
Alive with characters that never frown
Filled with music and art
With folk full of heart

Painting fine tapestries
Of life's past tragedies
Singing songs of the sea
To a bodhran's melody

Filling of bars packed tight
Jokes shared with a pint
Couples sit together
Ready for the singing on an open mic night

You will never be alone
Or feel forlorn,
As the folk who live here
Will make you feel right at home.

                                                Pureheart Wolf

Folk's Tales

THE SEARCH FOR SCOTTISH GIANTS

"I swear, there'd better be some girls when we get back to that village. Being out in the middle of nowhere with you two really makes a guy think about what he's missing. I have needs." Niles Grantham's sharp features were turned downwards as he spoke, the words echoing emptily around the gargantuan trunks of the trees surrounding them.

"Christ, Niles," Fred Harper replied, stoking the campfire. Its warmth wasn't quite enough to beat the ceaseless cold of the Scottish Highlands. "Thank god I've eaten my dinner."

"Thank God I don't have to share a tent with a horny adolescent," Chris Gray added brightly, smirking at Niles over the rim of the plastic beaker of whisky he was holding.

The three men were thickly swaddled in their outdoor gear, hats jammed over their ears and scarves pulled up high. Fred was from Texas, and even in four layers, he couldn't get used to the incessant bite in the air. It was damp, constantly. The first three days, he had been worried that their recording equipment would simply give up, but it seemed to be working. When the three men had huddled around the monitor in Chris' tent a few hours ago, they had watched the footage of their journey deep into the ancient, untamed Caledonian Forest.

Niles' camerawork was excellent: sweeping, breathtaking shots of the region that captured the otherworldly beauty of this place, while also evoking the unsettling loneliness Fred had felt since they left civilisation behind in Tyndrum.

(Privately, Fred thought that a village with a population of just over 150 people barely counted as civilisation. In this endless pine forest, though, where he had only seen two other human faces for days, he would have given anything to return to the tiny, picturesque place.)

The two tents and crackling bonfire looked like toys in comparison to the staggering pine trees surrounding them and extending far past the horizon, thickly covering the rolling hills. It made sense that Scotland had a rich history of stories about giants; everything about this place seemed designed for creatures far larger than man.

Fred had been fascinated by giants since childhood. His mother used to joke it was because he was such a short child, but his father maintained the family simply watched The Iron Giant one too many times. Neither parent felt surprised when Fred specialised in the psychology of folklore, with a focus on giants, during his studies.

"I might go to sleep," Niles said, draining his whisky. "Another night in the finest accommodation Scotland has to offer." His tone was wry.

"Sleeping under the stars in a place untouched by man," Chris replied. "I can think of worse things, Niles."

Niles uncurled himself from the fireside like a sleepy cat, stretching languidly. He was the youngest of the three men, barely in his twenties. In the amber glow of the fire, he looked like a child.

"You comin' to bed, boss?" he asked Fred.

Because Chris had so much more equipment than the other two, he slept alone in the smaller of the two tents, meaning Fred found himself sharing with the young cameraman. Niles snored, badly, but otherwise he wasn't bad company.

"Not yet. I was thinking I might look over more of the footage from the interviews, if Chris is up for it." Fred glanced over at Chris, who nodded.

"You know we're not being paid by the hour, right?" snorted Niles. "You already got the funding for the documentary, you know."

"They're sort of relying on us to make it, though," Chris observed.

"Suit yourselves. See you in the morning." Niles disappeared into the blue flap of the tent, closing it behind him.

Fred looked at Chris. "You ready to go look at some interviews?"

Chris led him into the other tent, which was on the other side of the clearing. The interior was illuminated by an eerie blue glow coming from the monitor, which Chris had set up on a folding table.

Due to the amount of equipment stuffed into the tent, there was no room for chairs. The two men squatted before the monitor. For a moment, there was the absolute silence that stalked them here. Chris broke it with a hollow laugh.

"I don't think Niles realises exactly how a documentary gets made," he said.

Fred shook his head. "I think he thought we'd see more, well, stuff. Giants' footprints, that sort of thing."

Chris looked at him. "Did you think we'd see that?"

"Well, no. But I wouldn't hate finding something like the Giant's Causeway here. Something we can talk about. At the minute we've got lots of interviews with weird old men in bars and shots of trees."

Chris didn't reply; instead clicked a button on the keyboard. The static blue screen was replaced by a wide shot of Fred sitting at a table in a pub opposite a red-faced gentleman.

"Can you introduce yourself for us?" asked the Fred on screen.

"My name's John McCraggan," said the old man in a thick, musical accent. "I used to be the bus driver, but I'm retired now."

"A bus driver! You must have-"

"Nah, lad. The bus driver. I was the only bus driver."

Fred on the monitor looked at the man for a second, then glanced helplessly at the camera, eyes clearly on the brink of rolling. There was the distinct sound of Niles snorting behind the camera, and then a strange, low sound like a laugh in the background.

Chris clicked the button to pause the recording. "I don't remember anyone laughing when we recorded this. We'll need to make sure we catch it when we clean the audio." He reached for his pen and notebook, ready to make a note of the required editing.

The laugh sounded again. Fred felt the hairs on the back of his neck, the ones currently hiding beneath his thick scarf, stand on end.

"It's not on the recording," he whispered.

Chris looked towards the entrance to the tent. They had closed it behind them. Fred was suddenly aware of how the thin sheet of plastic was all that currently stood between them and whatever had made that noise.

"We should go out," Chris said.

Neither man moved, though. The air was heavy with fears unvoiced by them. They sat perfectly still, barely breathing, waiting for that laugh to sound again.

It didn't.

"It must have been the recording equipment," Fred said unconvincingly. "Let's just… let's just watch the rest of the interview."

Chris looked at him, but he didn't speak. An agonising moment followed in which Fred wondered if Chris would refuse, but then he pressed play.

"We're here looking for giants," the Fred on the screen said.

"Giants, eh?" The old man's lips quirked up in a smile. "Not around here, laddie. You're much more likely to run into the baobhan sith."

"The what?"

"The baobhan sith. Vampire. Beautiful lassies who come and drink the blood of lonely men." The old man's grin was broader now, revealing a missing tooth. Fred felt his stomach sink.

"What makes you think that's more likely?" his on-screen avatar questioned, looking once again at the camera with a grimace.

"Lots of hikers have gone missing here. They probably wished for a female companion, if you catch my drift."

That unsettling laugh sounded in; it was joined by another. It was impossible to believe now that the sounds were coming from the recording. They seemed to be echoing around the tent, low and unnervingly gleeful. Chris reached to switch off the recording, but Fred caught his hand without thinking. He was staring at the old man.

"There's a Scottish superstition you might have heard of," John was saying now, "about making wishes at night. You can't do it without asking God's protection, and if you don't…"

Niles screamed in the other tent. It was a sound of pure suffering, short and shrill.

Fred's hand was still wrapped around Chris'. One of them had trembling fingers, and he didn't know who.

"Well," John continued cheerfully from the screen, "let's just say wishing for a lady lover at night is what invites the baobhan sith, and that's not what you want."

"I swear, there'd better be some girls when we get back to that village. Being out in the middle of nowhere with you two really makes a guy think about what he's missing. I have needs."

"Stop it," Fred whispered, and Chris turned the monitor off with his free hand.

The two men sat alone on the floor, fingers entwined, waiting.

A.R. Cole

Folk's Tales

JUGGLING WITH CYNTHIA NEPTUNE

Although I never met her, for a short while, Cynthia Neptune was my hero, but she didn't look like hero material at all. She was short, dumpy, a little overweight with slightly frizzy hair. She wasn't young and vigorous but when she stepped on a stage she created awe and respect. For Cynthia was a magician. And as befits a magician, she was gifted—courtesy of the local council—a summer season every year at the Panama Dip, Whitley Bay.

During the endless school summer holidays from around one thirty in the afternoon, the Panama Dip would begin to resemble a honey pot, with children homing in on it, accompanied by their parents, mostly mothers, mostly frazzled. Everyone wanted to be sure to get a good seat for the two o'clock start. The discerning audience would seek out the existing wooden seats dotted around the Panama Gardens and lay claim to them. The next best seats were on the higher levels of the concrete steps with a good view of the stage. After that, folding chairs from home might be set out but most people just brought blankets to cover the knobbly bits of ground. In any case it was impossible to expect children to stay in the same place so the entertainment was more promenade performance with buggies.

How we all admired Cynthia's purple jumpsuit adorned with moons and stars. This was the 1980s, not a decade known for its sober dressing, but none of us would have dared to wear such an outfit, even at a fancy dress party. At two o'clock prompt, Cynthia would confidently take up her place on the small podium which passed for a stage and—holding a microphone—would announce the beginning of the show to a chorus of whooping, clapping and stamping of feet. For some reason the magic show was never interrupted by older teenagers zipping around on bikes or roller skates. Maybe it just wasn't cool to even be seen there if you were over twelve.

So, the show would begin with singing and dancing by local stage schools. The sound system consisted of a microphone and two speakers so the singers had to sing loud, and the dancers had to not jump too much. However as the space was relatively small, this seemed to work. And how could you be disappointed when the sun was shining, you had a chance to sit down, your kids would be entertained and the entertainment was free!

Cynthia was more than equal to any man including her husband Johnny (also a magician). There were no rabbits in hats in her show, no doves rising above the Spanish City Dome. But there were many tricks which defied explanation and there was much audience participation. At Cynthia's request for volunteers, dozens of children would yank their hands above their ears and beg to be picked. Who would like to take part in the Indian Rope Trick, or help pull yards of silk bunting from their sleeves? Were there any volunteers for the milk bottle trick (where milk was mysteriously extracted from the assistant's arm)? Occasionally there'd be balloon modelling, after which a lucky child would go home with a rubber dachshund, hoping not to burst it on the way. And if children weren't picked there was always the hope that they might be, the following day.

After Cynthia had performed in the first half there would be a 'talent spot.' Usually this was taken up by shy children being dragged onstage by one of their parents, only to sing off-key. Gangly girls would perform a song with their friends, which usually ended in giggles as they regularly forgot the words or were too overawed by being on stage. Occasionally an overconfident boy might tell risqué jokes only to be bundled off quickly by 'security'—generally one of the older boys from the stage school. But sometimes there was the 'wow' factor when a child with real talent performed. One year one of my younger relatives stilled even the most fractious child as she sang the Michael Jackson song, 'Ben.'

As a mother of two with limited resources, I was glad to have been part of the happy bubble that was the Cynthia Neptune Magic Show at the Panama Dip. Like most people attending, although collectively we didn't look deprived, we were just about managing. The show was a brief interlude from life's worries about energy, mortgages and food bills, and a time of bonding with your children.

It wasn't until many years later that I found out via the local press that Cynthia's husband Jonny, had had a life-limiting condition. Although he worked full time as a magician, she worked as a bank clerk in order to save enough money for a time when it was inevitable that Jonny would have to give up his career. But when Jonny died young, Cynthia had her time in the limelight, quite literally. In her mid-fifties she became the most successful female northern children's entertainer, sometimes presenting thirty shows a week. At the height of her powers she became the first woman president of the Northern Magic Circle. And knowing all that, she rises even more in my estimation. At a time when women were fighting for equal pay and better working conditions, Cynthia forged her own unique and magical path.

As she watched us from the small stage at the centre of the Panama Dip, I like to feel that she identified with us, metaphorically juggling responsibilities for homes and family. We were just about managing to get through the long summer holidays. And miraculously we kept those balls in the air. Just like Cynthia.

Noreen Rees

GIG TALE

Andy Murfield – Morph – and Simon Tellers were Colm Albion. Just, one at a time and never together. I should know. I'm Simon Tellers. Follow?

Albion played clubs, pubs and village halls around the country. He covered trad and revival folksongs on a battered old Fender and a Tanglewood. He cut a skinny-ish dash except when he was north of the Humber, where his belly was slightly rounder and his face fuller. Albion cited Richard Thompson as his main formative influence, unless it was Ry Cooder. When it was Ry Cooder a touch of Morph slipped in. When it was Richard there was a bit of me.

"There's this guitarist, Rod Somebody," said Morph, after a Lightworks gig late 2005, the last we played in the same physical space (that's important). "He's got a doppelganger, same name, also a musician, plays techno on the Continent. Sometimes the wrong one gets booked."

"They won't muddle us." I said, "The Original Lightworks and the Northern Lights: not the same at all."

"I'll always say we didn't have to split."

"Shartistic differences. The decision's already been made."

It had, tempestuously. Nick Tumbrill, vocal lead, and Rory Ling, lead guitar, whose songs Nick had made his own, had fallen violently out. They were about to launch rival bands. Morph and I, holding no particular torch for either, had ended up one in each. This gig was a booking we couldn't afford the financial hit to get out of, so frosty that the backing singers nursed hypothermia.

"What if –" said Morph. "Let's have a bit of fun. They'll never tolerate it if we play together again. But say we shared a nom de guerre? Sometimes you'd play, sometimes me, different parts of the country, same playlist. See how long we can keep it going before people cotton on?"

With cameras, YouTube and MySpace, I gave it a fortnight. But it could be glorious chaos. So Colm Albion stepped onto stage.

There's a taste you get under your tongue, before you set sail the evening's first song. You're all wired up. Everything around you is vibrant, electrical. And suddenly it's like the root of your tongue has St Elmo's fire. That's when you know the gig will be good.

My first night as Albion, he had already played Hastings. Morph said he had gone down pretty well. He ended his five-song set picking out Guthrie's 'Vigilante Man', before ceding the stage for the main act.

I wondered, what were the odds up here outside Darlington, that anyone at that gig would also be at this? Truth was, alongside the taste of electricity I was getting a light imposter note, a hint of sulphurous mouldy lemon. I scanned the crowd for accusation. But in the dark, nothing came back at me. Relaxing, and on the spur replacing song one for two, I struck into 'Walk Awhile'. And it was good. It wasn't brilliant. But it was good.

Maybe the fact that we never went for headline slots, and we played deliberately in down-at-heel, dowdy halls, kept the photographs to a minimum, the deception under cover. Into the next decade, twelve alternate nights a year between us, maintaining a raggedy South/North divide, Morph and I cracked open our guitar cases and spilled out the Colm Albion playlist. Protest, wistful songs, retro-industrial romance, but never far from a standard like 'Dirty Old Town'. We didn't want Albion to draw much attention to himself, especially with Tumbrill and Ling still feuding.

The Original Lightworks and Northern Lights plodged middling paths through the silting estuary that was post-nineties indie-rock. In the late nineties, Lightworks had just about broken through. By 2005 we were broken. At first, after the split, both Tumbrill and Ling strove for a renaissance each felt they deserved. But I can tell you, for Northern Lights and our tribe, aspiration had lowered all too quickly into fixes of nostalgia, and I gathered from Morph, when we met, that the same was true for his band. It didn't help that Tumbrill couldn't write lyrics. Or that Ling, even when I tried to coach him, couldn't hold a tune.

I remember once, the day of the Brexit vote, standing outside the Playhouse at Whitley Bay. Two posters, side by accidental side, promoted The Ultimate Britpop Party and the Indie Garage Ball. The upcoming nights were two months and only inches apart. Appealing to the same crowd. Our bands in smallest font, beneath line-ups of groups that had one-time supported Pulp and Suede. Colm Albion could do better, I thought.

But Albion did covers, not originals. You write from experience: I guess, outside of each gig, he had none of that. And Morph and I were oddly venerating of him. We kept him pure. We made sure we partook of nothing about him outside each venue, save rehearsal time and the solicitation of the next performance. I never brought a girl home after a session. I was absolutely sure Morph didn't either. It's Folk, not Rock – and besides, weren't we getting old?

In 2020, of course, all touring stopped. In this hiatus, Tumbrill went weird. Each new conspiracy, said Morph, he was faster into it than Alice chasing rabbits under Watership Down. Perhaps the Knights Templar were still abroad, seeding virus vaccines via pages of holy copy. Or, as he claimed in January 2021, Corona had been hiding in plain sight in the name of the nation's favourite soap opera since 1960, only six years after the first Bilderberg Meeting, and surely that said all that needed to be said about Mainstream Media?

Something deeply private must have happened, but he ensured that the unravelling of his psyche was a public affair. Briefly, he was as famous as he'd ever wanted to be. The Northern Lights watched on Twitter, aghast and side-split, as his tweets gained traction. He formed a pressure group with a far right following. Morph Zoomed me late in 2022 to tell me that the Original Lightworks felt hobbled, and the drummer had left, but that he would hang in there, because Nick needed someone to look out for him, and anyway, Iceni Prime didn't pay their drivers enough.

I said, "We'll get Colm Albion back on the road."

Morph said, "That'll trouble the taxman."

And then it was Autumn, when everything changed.

One thing that should have tipped me off: midway through a tricksy 'Matty Groves' at my Albion gig at Padiham Town Hall, in the dark back of the room surely that wasn't Tumbrill, eyes snared with mine in a moment of mutual recognition? The man turned, exited the hall. When I looked again, the door had swung shut. It was probably wrong that I said nothing about it.

Because a month later, late in the night after Morph's last Albion gig, I got this panicked phone call:

"Simon, is anyone with you?"

"No." I said. "Morph?"

"Simon: shit, I —"

The sudden taste of off lemon. "Morph: whatever's just happened, tell me slowly."

Morph drew his breath. "I've driven into Nick."

Tumbrill had confronted him after the gig. He'd gone expecting to see me and seen Morph instead. Furious, he had waited for him outside the pub's back entrance, pinned him to the wall with the Fender's guitar case.

"He was at Padiham," I said. "Why did he go to Padiham?" Suddenly I was suspicious. "Did you let on I'd be there?"

"I've told no-one about Albion. Ever," said Morph. "Look: last month the Originals were playing the Burnley Mechanics Theatre. Nick got there a night early. He was looking for something close by to do. He thought Colm Albion sounded the kind of flag-humping patriot he'd like. He thought he saw you on stage, so this month he went to another gig to make sure. And he sees me. He was raging, Simon. He was going to blow our cover. We'd neither of us have worked with the bands again. You can't make a career as half-a-hippy playing covers."

"So you ran him over."

"My car hit him. It was an accident. I've cleaned it. No evidence. And I reported a body, so no poor dog-owner has to find it."

Why the taste of lemon again? "When you spoke to the police, did you give a name?"

Pause. "Colm Albion."

Which would be the end, except that I turned up for Albion's next gig. His life was there for me to step into. The police were waiting too, and quietly walked Colm off at the interval. I admitted to death by dangerous driving, leaving the scene of the crime.

Because Teller disappeared, and with Tumbrill gone, Rory Ling relaunched Lightworks with Morph as lead singer. If anyone else in that band notices Albion's resemblance to their erstwhile guitarist, well, music's cut-throat and the lighting's always bad.

I write original songs based on prison experience. A girl who knew Colm when he played in the South comes to visit.

Steve Lancaster

EVENSONG

The Earth's embrace
Its fierce grip, holds the mighty craftsmen;
They are perished and gone.
   anon. C8th

Five hundred years on, they allowed for giants,
Just to make sense of the crumbling walls.
What might we conjure, after our tyrants,
To explain the ruins, when our Babel falls?

Silicon cities under the waters,
Gleaming in nymph light through gas-curdled skies,
Fragments of plastic the scientists brought us,
Words that they taught us to trade for the wise,

Anvils the size of the smallest of fairies
To palpate the atoms and cleave DNA,
A deal with Cthulhu to dust-bowl the prairies,
And sirens are golden to lull and allay.

Picture a child at the end of the evening;
Rome is but shadows, long in the grass.
Our history's rich, but just tales to be weaving,
And who knows the worlds that will next come to pass?

Steve Lancaster

THE BOOK

So, I'm what you might call a fairytale hunter. Well, of sorts. I seek local legends and folklore. I bend the stories, twist them to my whim - rip out the dull and sew them back together into my own beautifully-crafted fairytales. The tales are new, shiny and happily-ever-after. From the old must always come the new. So I thought. So I believed. So reckless was I.

You see, not everyone has taken so kindly to me updating their old long-held legends. Some grew angry and bore threats. I laughed them off. Jealous, stick-in-the-mud hypocrites, I thought. And anyway, controversy was great for sales. I ignored the feeling, the reason those folk tales *meant* so much. Maybe that's why it happened. Maybe that's why I ended up finding something I should never have been allowed to touch. Folklore is like a precious memory held in time and carried through to those who never lived it. Maybe it alters with time a little, the details muddle, but the *message*, the *warning*, is the same. Stories, I had forgotten, are their own creatures – with the power to swallow you whole.

The press thing had been getting steadily worse. Angry letters, phone calls and all the online visceral trolling my media manger could handle. So I took a break; went off-grid. Somewhere up north... I found a little town not far from Chillingham Castle. I could probably find some nice folklore for my next book while I was there.

I don't think the locals knew who I was – they didn't seem to read much, knowing very few of the titles I mentioned – or if they did, they didn't seem to care. There wasn't much in the way of nightlife except the local pub, but the people were friendly and welcomed me with a smile. It's always good to fish around with a friendly smile; find out what local lore is still in-play. Mostly it was the usual 'touch wood' to stave off bad luck, turning your clothes inside-out if you get lost in a forest and so on. There was a tale of a local witch, but it wasn't much to work with. I wasn't getting much done but I was enjoying reading all day, hiding myself in fantasy then ending my day with a pint and a chat. Let someone else deal with reality for a while.

I'd only been there a few days when I saw it one evening on my way to the pub. A small crooked door, propped open, the light in the room so dim it looked like it was lit by a single candle. The walls seemed to bow outwards as if buckling under the history of its ancient stones. Inside was a tiny and crammed-to-the-rafters bookshop. I couldn't believe no-one else was in there when I went in. Maybe the locals were so used to it they didn't bother. I chose a particularly beautiful red leather-bound book with a golden key on the front and a clasp at the side. If I'm honest, I didn't even glance at the inside, it just looked so nice that I fell in love with the romance of it. If I didn't like the writing, I could just use it as a paperweight. The cashier was a woman with pale skin and dark hair, which was starting to show the first flecks of silver. She smiled so broadly as I placed the book on the counter. She began to wrap the book without a word.

"Quiet evening," I offered.

"Yes. Good for reading. Two pounds please." Her voice was a like a low breath, barely audible. And the price, wow!

"It's lovely in here. A real hidden gem. I thought there would be more people. So reasonably-priced too!"

"Yes, the village folk are not much for reading, as you already know, I'm sure… I do hope you enjoy getting lost in that book. It's not for everyone."

"I'm sure I will. Thanks. I'll see you again tomorrow."

"Perhaps. Goodnight."

There was a chill in the air as I walked on to the pub. I shivered and considered skipping my evening drink and going straight back to the cottage, but I hadn't eaten and there was still plenty of time. The rush of warmth when I opened the pub door did nothing to relieve the cold that now tingled inside me. I sat by the fire with my pint but still felt cold and even the delicious homemade shepherd's pie didn't bring the heat back to my bones.

Adam, a very friendly farmer I'd chatted to before, sat by me.

"How-do, how goes the holiday?"

"Great thanks, how long has that book shop been"

His face went pale and all the friendly playfulness dropped away. He shook his head.

"No, you don't want to go in there. It's a…"

"Too late! I already splashed out a whole two pounds."

"No!"

"It's just a book."

"Nothing is *'just'* anything. You need to stay grounded. People round here, we know, we know you can't let yourself get taken by someone else's dreams…"

"Oh really, Adam. What harm can a little escapism do?"

"You can lose yourself, that's what. That book, it'll… You'll lose your grip on what's real. Reading too much - it's not healthy. Books are portals, you don't know where it might lead you."

OK. That was a new one. I realised the whole pub had silently paused. All eyes were on Adam and I.

"Please promise me you won't read it."

I felt as if the room had taken a collective in-breath and was holding it for us. Adam was unblinking, a pleading look in his eyes. When I nodded it was as if someone had hit the reset button. Everyone began chatting and moving again. Adam smiled and relaxed back into his chair. What utter nonsense! The rest of the evening continued on as usual, calm and jolly. I made a mental note to gently investigate later how this local aversion to reading had been born. Not tonight though. After chatting a while I made my way back to the cottage.

I reached in my bag; the book felt cool against my fingers. I lit a fire and added an extra fleece to my outfit, then finished my notes on the locals' behaviour. A seductive call to imagination tugged at me. I was alone; alone with my new book. I took it out to read. I held it close to my bare skin, touching it to my forehead. The book felt warm in my hands, as if it were living; as if, just by touching it, *I* gave it life. I *had*

Folk's Tales

to read it. Had to explore just a few pages. The prospect of the tales within was so enticing; magic adventures, a perfect world.

I looked over the stories, letting myself freefall into fiction. I could have stopped after the first few pages, but I greedily drank in each word, forgetting my promise.

I sat transfixed by the words of a thousand years, missing the world spinning, whirling and disappearing around me. I let myself swim with selkies and fly with dragons. My limbs grew light and I didn't notice I was being stolen. I could smell the sulphur of the dragon's breath, feel the bark of the trees of enchanted forests, saw magic dance before my eyes. I felt myself almost dropping, as if off to sleep, but my eyes were still open. Slowly, gently, falling into fiction, I looked to turn the page but it was gone. I looked up.

Around me, the perfect fairytale worlds I'd once dreamed of now surrounded me like a prison. A prison I'd built myself. Selkies clawing at my legs, dragons scorching my skin, nymphs knotting my hair as tree sprites tore at my clothes. And my name. What was my name? Did I have one? When you become part of the story, you see, you are the story. I couldn't, *can't* leave this book. I was, *am* trapped between the pages of a tale of my own making. But worst of all... I can feel the dreaded darkness of my book's covers being slowly closed. Someone, please, help me and write me a happy ending...

Elizabeth Drabble

CONTRIBUTORS

Bea Charles writes short fiction and articles for publication, fillers for cash, and flash fiction for fun. She has been published in several UK magazines including Writers' Forum, Mslexia and Woman's Weekly and is a regular contributor to ParagraphPlanet.com. She blogs (occasionally and alphabetically) at https://beacreativewriter.wordpress.com.

James A. Tucker is a neurodivergent human who has survived more than fifty orbits of Sol. He lives in the north hemisphere with a feline overlord and does a lot of over- and under-thinking. Find him online at https://paladinofidleness.wordpress.com.

Harry Gallagher is a widely published poet, with several books available. He has written poetry commissions for the BBC, Northern Rail and The Great North Museum. He runs the Tyne & Wear stanza of The Poetry Society and is on the poetry editorial team of The Morning Star. www.harrygallagherpoet.wordpress.com.

Penny Blackburn's work has featured in many journals and anthologies, including Leicester Writes, Spelt, Riggwelter and Phare and she was the winner of Poetry Tyne 2023. She has released her debut collection with Yaffle Press, Gaps Made of Static. She is on Facebook as @Penbee8.

Missi Currier is an excitable anarcho-nuisance who likes to write about people, ecology, and a weird brutalist high rise she used to call home. She lives in the North East of England, where she likes to stare into rockpools and is often seen being followed by a large flock of crows.

Jennifer C. Wilson is co-founder and current host of North Tyneside Writers' Circle. She writes a range of fiction and non-fiction, published through Ocelot Press, and has recently been working on developing her poetry. She can frequently be found stalking dead monarchs. Find her on X as @inkjunkie1984.

Jessica Arragon has been reading her whole life. She writes for herself, having bursts of activity followed by spells of nothing at all. Jessica has been attending NTWC for a couple of years. She enjoys the creative space, the work of others and the opportunity to step outside of her writing comfort zone with the prompts shared.

Ross Punton is a writer from South Shields, on the autistic spectrum, which gives him a unique world view. A keen runner he loves being out by the coast where he lives. His poetry is humorous and anecdotal. He supports and loves the spoken word community in the North East.

Wayne Medford writes both poetry and non-fiction. He is a member of Cullerpoets, and North Tyneside Writers' Circle. He is a member of the North East Group of the Society of Authors.

Joss Hancock is an English Literature and Creative Writing grad, as well as an amateur actor, songwriter, singer, and sucker for all things spooky.

Renata Connors is a poet and songwriter based in Tynemouth, Tyne & Wear. Her poems are published in various webzines. She has performed her poetry and songs at many different venues around the North East. She likes learning and teaching languages. Some of her song lyrics can be found here: https://renataconnors.bandcamp.com.

Alexi Calamity is an award-winning short story writer who also designs puzzles & games, scripts comics, draws comics, exhibits in galleries, DJs, and dances like a dafty. More info: alexiconman.blogspot.com.

Arthur J. Montieth is a now-retired adult computer trainer and business advisor. Born in Newcastle he is now living in North Shields. He has a wide range of interests in science, politics and computing. He writes stories as a hobby. Find him online at https://www.facebook.com/arthur.montieth.

Alison Sidney enjoys writing flash fiction and short stories which evolved from entering slogan competitions. The discipline of writing slogans in twelve words or less definitely helped in the editing process of longer work. Though she does miss the excitement of the post bringing the news of a slogan win which included food hampers, a trip to Dublin, several cases of wine, and a car.

Bridget Gallagher writes poetry and short stories and lives at the seaside with her husband and Alfie the whippet. When not writing, she can be found playing the concertina or trying to beat her grandsons at chess. She loves to sing and helps run a sea shanty group. www.positivelyup.co.uk.

Jenny Smith lives in Whitley Bay. Her work focuses on family histories, her north east heritage, and her bohemian upbringing. She is fascinated by the stories we tell ourselves. She runs a monthly spoken word event, is a member of the team behind Whitley Bay Poetry Trail, and has supported other participatory arts projects. Instagram @towritesomethingofvalue

Chris Longstaff is a North Shields native who in-between cooking chickens, daydreaming and watching films, somehow finds the time to write short stories, comics and feature length scripts. He has been known to specialise in a witty comment or two. X: @ComicChris13.

Pureheart Wolf is an admin and moderator for a number of writing groups on Facebook, and is based in North Shields. She has had work published in anthologies across England and America.

A.R. Cole is a silly and whimsical little bundle of anxiety and adventure. She is in her thirties and, if cut, bleeds hummus and glitter. Find her on X @absolutelycole.

Noreen Rees is a member of Carte Blanche women's writing group, and as well as writing poetry has also had two children's books published, and several short stories. She is also a playwright – plays performed include Not Some Kind of Sideshow (Northumberland Theatre Company). She has worked as a writer on community projects for several organisations. www.facebook.com/noreen.rees.

Steve Lancaster is a poet writing and performing in the north east. He cartoons and designs boardgames under the name Weirdly Bay. Find out more at https://linktr.ee/Steve_Lancaster.

Elizabeth Drabble has been writing for a few years now. Currently working on a collection of twisted Fairy tales. Elizabeth spends most of her time gardening with her husband.

Images:
NTWC logo – Jim Hubbard.
Cover photo – Missi Currier.
Other photos – Penny Blackburn, Missi Currier, Elizabeth Drabble, Jenny Smith, James A. Tucker, Jennifer C. Wilson.

Edited by Jennifer C. Wilson & the editorial committee.

www.facebook.com/NorthTynesideWritersCircle

Folk's Tales